Uncle Bill

LOOK-SEE
WITH UNCLE BILL

LOOK-SEE
WITH UNCLE BILL

BY WILL JAMES

WITH DRAWINGS BY THE AUTHOR

MOUNTAIN PRESS PUBLISHING COMPANY
MISSOULA, MONTANA
2002

First Printing, July 2002

Mountain Press Publishing Company changed a few words in *Look-See with Uncle Bill* that are offensive to modern society. Mountain Press made the changes with the permission of the copyright holder and with the view that many titles of the Tumbleweed Series are purchased for school libraries.

*Tumbleweed Series is a registered trademark
of Mountain Press Publishing Company.*

Library of Congress Cataloging-in-Publication Data

James, Will, 1892–1942.
    Look-see with Uncle Bill / by Will James ; with drawings by the author.
        p. cm. — (Tumbleweed series)
Summary: While spending their summer vacation with Uncle Frank and Uncle Bill, two city children discover and begin to explore what seems to be an old gold mine shaft, but find that it is guarded by mountain lions.
    ISBN 0-87842-459-8 (alk. paper) — ISBN 0-87842-458-X (pbk. : alk. paper)
    [1. Cowboys—Fiction. 2. Ranch life—Fiction. 3. Puma-Fiction. 4. Gold mines and mining—Fiction. 5. West (U.S.)—Fiction.] I. Title.
PZ7.J1545 Lo 2002
[Fic]—dc21

2002007627

PRINTED IN CANADA

Mountain Press Publishing Company
P.O. Box 2399 • Missoula, Montana 59806
406-728-1900

PUBLISHER'S NOTE

WILL JAMES'S BOOKS are an American treasure. His writing and drawings captivated generations of readers with the lifestyle and spirit of the American cowboy and the West. Following James's death in 1942, the reputation of this remarkable writer and artist languished, and nearly all of his twenty-four books went out of print. But in recent years, publication of several biographies and film documentaries on James, public exhibitions of his art, and the formation of the Will James Society have renewed interest in his work.

Now, in conjunction with the Will James Art Company, Mountain Press is reprinting all Will James's books under the name the Tumbleweed Series, taking special care to keep each volume faithful to the original. Books in the Tumbleweed Series contain all the original artwork and text, feature an attractive new design, and are printed on acid-free paper.

The republication of Will James's books would not have been possible without the help and support of the many fans of Will James. Because all James's books and artwork remain under copyright protection, the Will James Art Company has been instrumental in providing the necessary permissions and furnishing artwork.

The Will James Society was formed in 1992 as a nonprofit organization dedicated to preserving the memory and works of Will James. The society is one of the primary catalysts behind a growing interest not only in Will James and his work, but also in the life and heritage of the working cowboy. For more information on the society, contact:

Will James Society • c/o Will James Art Company
2237 Rosewyn Lane • Billings, Montana 59102

Mountain Press is pleased to make Will James's books available again. Read and enjoy!

JOHN RIMEL

BOOKS BY WILL JAMES

Cowboys North and South, 1924

The Drifting Cowboy, 1925

Smoky, the Cowhorse, 1926

Cow Country, 1927

Sand, 1929

Lone Cowboy, 1930

Sun Up, 1931

Big-Enough, 1931

Uncle Bill, 1932

All in the Day's Riding, 1933

The Three Mustangeers, 1933

Home Ranch, 1935

Young Cowboy, 1935

In the Saddle with Uncle Bill, 1935

Scorpion, 1936

Cowboy in the Making, 1937

Flint Spears, 1938

Look-See with Uncle Bill, 1938

The Will James Cowboy Book, 1938

The Dark Horse, 1939

Horses I Have Known, 1940

My First Horse, 1940

The American Cowboy, 1942

TO
KIP POWERS
A TOP HAND
OF THE FOURTH GENERATION
OF THE COWBOY
I DEDICATE THIS BOOK

PREFACE

A FINE SUNSET can be looked at and not appreciated enough to really be seen. A horse track crossing a trail might be looked at the same, and to most it's only a horse track, but with the range rider he sees that the horse might either be drifting on to other ranges or was being ridden.

There's many things that's looked at but not really seen, nor appreciated because they're not understood and so, sometimes hardly noticed.

With this story of Kip and Scootie, two city kids on their third summer at a big ranch in the heart of the cow country and under the watchful eagle eye of an old cowboy called Uncle Bill they get to look and really see, by that learn and understand as they ride with him or work by his coaching.

They get stumped a few times but the old cowboy, most always on hand, sees that they learn with every happening, learn things that young and older folks who've never been in the rough and open country and weather will also learn as Kip and Scootie did, by seeing with Uncle Bill.

It's a look-see from the open spaces that can well fit with the teachings of closed in spaces.

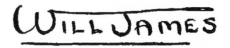

ILLUSTRATIONS

LOOK-SEE
WITH UNCLE BILL

CHAPTER ONE

"LOOK!" SCREAMED A HAPPY VOICE. "That's my saddle on that little black horse."

"And see!" screamed another happy voice. "It's my saddle on the little gray right next to him."

The happy voices was from two kids, a boy and a girl, who had just stepped off a west-bound train onto the wooden platform of a little depot that needed only two men to hold down. One of the men was now wheeling in the kids' trunk. The few people that had come to watch the train pull in and out again wandered back to what there was of the town,—only a small cow town that didn't show much life until shipping time, in the fall and when big herds of cattle was drove in to be loaded into train after train of stock cars and shipped to markets.

The kids, after making sure it was their saddles they was looking at, also their saddle blankets under 'em and their bridles on the horses' heads both got to wondering, they'd never seen the two horses before, they wasn't any of the ones they'd been used to riding, and looking up and down the platform they wondered some more at why there was nobody to meet them. Every spring before, when they'd come West for the summer, there'd always been a couple of grinning big-hatted cowmen to catch 'em as

1

They'd never seen the two horses before.

soon as they come off the train. One was their Uncle Frank, and the other was an old cowboy nicknamed Uncle Bill on account of his knowledge and wisdom, and advice he would never give unless asked for. But old Uncle Bill had no known relatives, and he'd never hunted up any.

Uncle Frank was the real uncle of the kids. Frank had been born and raised on the big ranch that was his and which the kids had come to for the summer. They'd studied hard during the winter while at home in the big eastern city so as to make the grade and be allowed to come west during summers, and during their winters' learning they lived pretty well only for summer to come so they could get west and on their Uncle's ranch. Every day starting February, that being the shortest month, was crossed off and the ones following were counted. March was the worst on account of it being the longest, and then when the trees begin to bud in the city parks and grass begin to green it got to be worse yet. It was harder and harder for them to keep their minds on their schoolwork. The pages of their books would blur into visions of bands of horses running by, bunches of cattle grazing in high mountain meadows and the old cowboy, Uncle Bill, riding by their side and talking to them. If it wasn't that their parents had made it plain that there would be no summer West unless they qualified with their schooling, the kids would of been mighty apt to've fallen short in points. So, as it was, they'd grit their teeth and manage to make it by the skin of 'em.

This was their third summer to come West, and they'd got to feeling real western. And why shouldn't they? They'd been west and got to know some of it well, their dad was born West and raised on the same ranch their uncle Frank was and which they was now going to. Western blood was in their veins, and even tho their mother was an Eastern woman and raised in the big city there was pioneer blood in her veins too, and if her forefathers' could not of been traced back to the pioneers, or pilgrims, who came on the *Mayflower*, they was close second on some other boat. Anyhow there was no friction between the East and West in the Powers family.

It was Frank's brother Ben's choice to go East and go into business there instead of staying on the range. He done mighty well at it. "And that goes to prove" Frank often said "that he'd never been worth a hoot as a cowboy." Both was happy and successful at their own chosen profession. One a hard figuring architect and contractor and the other a hard riding cowman and ranch owner.

As for Old Uncle Bill, he'd been on the Powers' ranch, the Five Barb 5 for over twenty-five years, when Frank was still a youngster and riding broncs. He'd took deep root to the outfit and range, had been made foreman and was still on foreman's wages as the best and most valuable cowman the Five Barb ever had. He'd rode for many other horse and cow outfits thruout the western states and as far north and south as there was range and stock. But now the Five Barb was his home, he hadn't kept track of his accumulated wages, and that he never thought of, for his needs wasn't many. The amount of his wages could ride and grow with the outfit.

Now, during the summers since Kip and Scootie began coming west, he'd been asked to take charge of the kids and see they didn't get hurt or lost, something which the old cowboy didn't care much for at first, but that was at first.

The kids, at one end of the depot, sizing up the strange horses under their own saddles was very puzzled as to what was up. Each time before when they piled out of the train they'd been met by one or both of the uncles and a big car would be waiting which would whiz 'em the many miles to the ranch in no time, but now—Well, it was sure puzzling.

They looked up and down the depot platform, not a soul was in sight, then they went to the baggage room and finding the baggage man there the girl asked him if he knew about the two horses tied to the platform by the side of the depot and if he'd seen the men who'd tied 'em there.

The baggage man took time to go out the door, look at the horses and spit before he answered. "No," he says, "I didn't get to see who it was tied them there and I don't know the horses either, but," he went on, "you'd most likely easy find out by going acrost the street to the Palace Hotel. Some of the old lobby hounds there would most likely know."

The kids, still wondering, started acrost the wide street, one wide street where they didn't have to watch for traffic, but they hadn't got halfways across when two fast riding cowboys come to their sight sudden, like they'd shot up from the earth or dropped from the sky and raising a dust the size of a small cyclone. The kids, thinking the riders was on a spree, started on a run for the sidewalk and safety, but the street was too wide and before they could get there the two riders pulled up in front of 'em.

The kids stopped, stared up a little scared, but their expressions soon changed to joy, for the two riders was none other than the two uncles grinning down at 'em and looking sort of apologizing for not meeting them at the train. But the kids' happy smiles soon made them forget that.

"Fact is," says Frank, as him and Uncle Bill got down off their horses, "we was just in the middle of unloading a carload of bulls which I'd traded for and just came in, and I of course wanted to tally up on 'em." Then, with a pleased look as he sized up the kids, he went on. "By the eternal," he says, "you two have sure

Two fast riding cowboys come to their sight.

growed since I last seen you, must of been eating some of my beef out there in the big city."

"Yep," Uncle Bill chips in. "They're not sprouts no more but fair sized stems, and I'm thinking they'll have to let their stirrups out at least one hole before they go to riding again."

After the first flood of words at all meeting one another again the four started for the shade of the depot and where the other two horses was tied.

On the way, Frank glanced at the sun and remarked, "About four hours of daylight left. I guess there won't be no taking the bulls as far as Rock Creek today, as we'd planned. Maybe graze 'em on Murphy's ranch and stay there for the night. That's only six miles.

"You and Chuck can take 'em on that far," he says to Bill. "Me and the kids will help you start 'em out, then I'll come back with 'em, stay at the hotel for the night and we'll catch up with you and Chuck in the morning."

The kids was all ears to listening, trying to figure what their Uncle Frank was talking about and how they could get to know about the goings on without asking questions. But there was one thing they was sure of, and that's there was riding in the wind.

Then Uncle Bill spoke up. "I don't see why we can't just as well go on to Rock Creek," he says. "Them young bulls, after an hour or so of grazing and a little rest, will take to the trail like grease to a hot skillet. It'll be cool going during the night and the thirty miles there will only limber 'em up. You and the kids could catch up with me and Chuck there or a little further on tomorrow."

Frank agreed that that would be all right. Old Uncle Bill seemed always right. Then the four come to where the two horses was tied.

"There's your ponies," says Frank to the kids, "brand new ones."

The two uncles of course was expecting signs of glad surprise on the kids' faces, and they wasn't at all disappointed. The kids just sort of rolled their eyes at 'em and grinned wide. They couldn't say a word. But the expressions on their faces showed a plenty and words couldn't of expressed how they felt.

Finally the boy walked to the horse that had his saddle on, the gray, touched him on the neck and run his fingers thru the silky mane.

"Gee, he's pretty," he says.

At that there was a comment come by the little black which had the girl's saddle on. "Not any prettier than mine," she says.

"Well, I wouldn't trade you," says the boy.

"Neither would I," come the quick retort.

The two uncles looked at one another and grinned. "I guess we didn't make no mistake picking them out to taste," says the oldest one.

Getting close to the horses and looking them over well was as far as they could get for the time being, for as the boy went to untie his horse and get on him, his Uncle Frank spoke up.

"Not yet, Kip," he says. "No use getting your creased city clothes all mussed up. You'll need 'em again when you go back this fall."

The girl had been about to get on her horse too, regardless of skirt and silk stockings, but thought better of it as she heard her uncle speak to Kip. Her uncle went on.

"You kids have got the clothes you used out here with you, haven't you? I remember you always used to take 'em along, maybe to smell the horse on 'em when you're home."

"Yes. We have them," says the girl, smiling.

"All right then, give me the check for your baggage and I'll have it taken up to the Hotel, where you can change to clothes more fitting to the saddle."

It didn't take long to get the baggage to the Hotel. Tying all four horses to the station platform, they went to the agent, borrowed the cart and in a jiffy the trunk and cases was transferred to the Hotel, to be picked up there by a couple of bellhops and hoisted to a couple of rooms.

"Now, go to it, kids," says Frank. "While you change your clothes I'll go help Bill and Chuck start the bulls out of the yards and I'll come back after you."

"You don't need to do that," says the old cowboy. "Them is quiet bulls, and me and Chuck can start 'em without any trouble." Then he looked at the kids and grinned, "Better stay with them," he says; "they look right now as if they're afraid you'd be deserting 'em for good if you went."

That settled it. Frank stayed, and there was a rush for the trunk and cases. Boots, spurs, overalls, ropes and hats and more stuff fitting to the range was being jerked out, then Kip, with his uncle in one room and the girl in another, went to making a fast change. No quick change artist could of changed any quicker. Then, as the city clothes was being put in the place of the ones they now wore, there come a sort of hesitating look to Kip's face, like he wanted to ask something and was afraid to for fear of being refused. Frank noticed the look and asked.

"What's troubling you, Kip, forget something?"

"No, he says; "I was just wondering."

"Wondering what?"

"Well," Kip was now in for it, "I was wondering if I could go along with Uncle Bill and Chuck to Rock Creek. I'm all ready now and I would sure like to be out riding instead of staying in a stuffy room. I had enough of staying inside last winter."

Frank thought on the subject a while and it didn't surprise Kip much when he spoke.

"But it'll be an all night ride, boy. You must be tired from the trip. This would be too long a ride to start with, and besides it's going to be chilly and it looks like it's going to storm and—"

Frank would of went on some more, and Kip might of lost out in his plea, when the girl who'd overheard some of the talk from the adjoining room busted in and spoke up without any hesitating and in a way that nipped in the bud all that Frank might of had in his mind against the kids starting right out on the long night ride.

But she had the advantage on her Uncle Frank from the start, for instead of coming out in overalls as she had before she was all togged up in a neat riding skirt of colt hide, with a vest to match, and new neat fitting handmade boots. She made a picture that was sure worth looking at, and Frank was doing just that, hardly hearing a word she was saying.

He got the drift somehow that she was backing up what her brother Kip had said, and that she was all for getting out too and get the city and railroad soot and grime out of her eyes and system. And with the anxious expressions in her face and Kip's he had to give in.

"All right, all right," he grinned, throwing up both hands; "you win. But I'll tell you," he went on, "you children will have to have some warmer clothes. The nights are mighty chilly yet and you never can tell what kind of weather or trouble we might bump into before we get to the other end. I have a car coming in to get you and your stuff tomorrow, and I wish you two would stay here tonight and go in it to the ranch instead of coming along on the drive. I only wanted to surprise you with the horses and give you a short ride and was going to lead them back."

"No, sir." Both kids spoke at once, and Frank seen there was no use in talking.

"All right," he said again; "let's go then and get them clothes and we'll all ride. The last one out is a drag, a no account wind-belly."

But there was no drags, for all three, laughing and crowding, hit the door at the same time.

CHAPTER TWO

A T THE BIG GENERAL STORE which had supplied the stockmen for more than sixty miles around and carried most everything, from postage stamps to flour and bacon and galloway coats, etc., is where Frank took the kids in and started fitting them out. It was kind of hard to get the sizes of what was needed, but finally they both of 'em was rigged up in pretty fair fitting mackinaw coats, also slickers,—not the regular pommel slicker, for there was none near small enough,—the plain, straight slicker would have to do.

Then Frank, seeing Kip looking at some shaps[1] that was hanging on the wall, went near him and also looked up at them. There was all kinds, plain leather batwings, some fancy ones, then some angoras and bear.

"That's right, by Christopher, you haven't got no shaps, have you, Kip? Well, here's where we rig you up in a pair."

The girl came along about that time, and seeing what was going on, she remarked: "Gee whiz, Uncle Frank, a person would think we're going to the North Pole the way you're rigging us up. We got along without all this before."

---

[1]Shaps; short for chaparejos, leather leggings or covering, some with fur on outside of leg.

"Yes, but you was tucked right into a car and drove right on to the ranch where you could soon find shelter and where you didn't have to be out if it stormed, but this is different. If you want to go along with the cattle you'll have to be out rain or shine, snow or sleet, and any of that kind of weather often comes this time a year. This outfit will come in handy for you, spring and fall and often in the summer when up in the mountains. I guess you know that. Besides, Kip ought to be rigged up some to be riding alongside of you with that pretty riding skirt you're wearing."

Finding a long willow with a hook at the end of it and which the store keeper used to get goods down with, Frank asked Kip what pair he'd like to look at. Kip didn't hesitate, he pointed at a plain pair of split-cowhide batwings with not an ornament on it or even a concho at the snaps.

"Why don't you pick out a pair of the pretty ones?" asked the girl. "The ones with the different colored leathers sewed in pretty designs, and buttons and fringe"

Kip hardly glanced at his sister as he answered, "That kind is all right for circuses where a feller has to wear 'em to hold his job, like loud-colored silk shirts and such, but not for me."

Frank, grinning to himself, took down the pair Kip had picked out and held 'em up against the boy. "By jiminy," he says; "they ain't much too long for you. A few inches cut off the bottom and they'll do fine till we get to the ranch and do the final trimming and adjusting. Doggone if they ain't of the same make as mine."

Back to the depot and to the horses the slickers and coats was tied on the saddles, then the horses was rode to the feed stable where they was watered, fed some grain and plenty of good hay.

A few inches cut off the bottom and they'll do fine.

"Well, now," says Frank, "we have plenty of time being we're going to ride all night, and we better feed up too. It might be a long time till next time."

The kids was too excited to be very hungry, but as they got to a close restaurant, and at Frank's advice, they sort of calmed down and got around a pretty fair feed once they got started.

Back at the stable, and to give the horses more time to eat, Frank told the kids that now would be a good time to let their stirrups out one hole. That's easier done while the saddle is on a horse, and with as gentle horses as the kids' was they'd keep right on eating, not at all disturbed.

Each with a marlinspike borrowed from the stable man the kids went to work unlacing the stirrup leathers, and seeing they was doing well, Frank, saying he'd forgot something at the store and telling them he'd be back in a short while, went out.

But his short while turned out to be quite a while, and when he got back, with a package which he wrapped in his slicker and tied on his saddle, the kids was about thru lacing back the stirrup leathers, one hole lower.

That done, and the horses watered once more, the three climbed into their saddles and started out of the little cow town.

"Prettiest time of the day, the evening," remarked Frank as he glanced at the sun; "like sun-up and the seasons of spring and fall. But right now," he went on, looking towards the eastern skyline, "it looks like we're due for a little wetting and I'm thinking you children will be initiating your slickers. Them thunder heads," he says, pointing at dark and solid looking little clouds, "are the leaders or advance scouts for a big army of clouds that'll be following up to swoop over the country with a heavy rain, maybe hail and sleet, and maybe snow. There'll most likely be a war band too, and that'll be with plenty of thunder and lightning along with all the dousing."

The kids looked at the little dark clouds, like on deploy and soaring fast. There must of been a strong wind up there to make them travel so, thought the kids, and they wondered why they didn't feel any as they rode. It was still, too still, and the girl thought of once reading some saying about the calm before the storm.

"It might miss us," says Frank as the three rode on, "but if it does hit us I'm thinking you kids will be wishing you'd stayed at the Hotel. . . . But it ain't too late to go back if you want, we're only out a couple of miles."

"Not by a durn sight," says Kip, right quick. "This horse feels too good under me. Let 'er rain, it'll be a good chance to initiate my new slicker, as you said. If it leaks it'll do me good and maybe loosen up my hide; it's been wedged in between brick walls for so long that I'm afraid it's drawing up on me."

"Well," Frank chuckled, as he looked at the thunder heads again, "I'm thinking it'll be moistened up all right." Then turning to the girl, "How about you, Scootie?" he asks. "Do you want to ride on, or—"

Frank didn't say no more as the girl Scootie looked at him, smiled happy-like and just said, "I feel the same as Kip does about it, for riding on and on."

Frank grinned, shrugged his shoulders and put his rangy bay to a trot, the kids glad to keep up alongside of him and see how their new outfits, horses and all, felt. Kip rode along looking down at his new shaps and seeing how well they hung, Scootie was doing the same about her new riding skirt, and Frank noticing 'em couldn't help but remark:

"Good thing there ain't no mirages you can see yourselves in or you'd be riding into 'em and getting lost."

At that he eased his horse into a long swinging lope, and then the kids got to paying more attention to their horses. The way their two smaller horses kept near even gait with their uncle's long legged bay pleased 'em mighty well, there was no jerky or choppy stride, for they was young, and even tho full of life and feeling good there was not a silly prance in 'em nor any up and down throwing of the head. Kip thought his gray was a honey of a lollapoloosa and Scootie had hers up as a dear of a humdinger.

"Well," grins Frank, as he heard the kids' remarks, "not to be outdone nor be left afoot as to compliments for the deserving I'll say for this cavayo[1] I'm riding that for splitting the breeze, cutting out of a herd, or roping he can't be beat. He's a tagamagoozler of a workadoo."

Feeling bested, the kids looked at him and smiled. "But what do you call him?" asks Scootie.

"I don't call him, I rope him when he won't let me walk up to him in a corral,—then of course I'm liable to call him a few other names. But the cowboy who broke him hung the whole name of Guadalupe on him. I guess that cowboy must of had a girl or made some winnings down there, anyhow I've renamed him Gumbo, because he's a sticker, and just so anybody would know which horse I'm talking about when I talk about him."

The three had slowed their horses down to a walk again thru the conversation, and then Frank remarked as to how there ought to be signs of the cattle pretty soon. And pretty soon there was. They was riding along the road when they come to tracks where

---

[1]Spanish—for horse.

17

the cattle had been drove along it for a ways and then turned off to the other side. Another mile or so further on and the bulls was seen quietly grazing in a grassy swale. The two saddled horses, hobbled and bits out of their mouths, was also grazing to their hearts' content, close to where Uncle Bill and Chuck was laying stretched out and resting for the night's ride that was ahead.

"You boys went right along," says Frank as him and the kids rode up on 'em.

"Yep," agreed Uncle Bill. "They wanted to run some as we turned 'em out of the railroad yards and we let 'em for a ways, but they sure wanted to travel and there was no let up much till we got here, the tall green grass stopped 'em. They ought to be all full up pretty soon the way they been eating, and then be laying down and go to chewing their cud."

"Yeh," says Frank, getting off his horse, "and I'll bet one of them bulls to a watermelon that you fellers didn't bring *yourselves* anything to chew on and that you didn't eat before leaving town either."

"You win," grins the old cowboy, "but you'll have to wait before I can pay my side of the bet because watermelons don't seem any too plentiful around here. But there is mushrooms, and I can gather you up a couple of hatfuls if that'll do."

Uncle Bill wasn't fooling about mushrooms. He pointed down the swale a short ways and there could be seen a good sprinkling of 'em showing thru the green grass. The past heavy rains had brought 'em on.

At the sight of 'em there was no stopping the kids from going over and picking some. They'd long ago learned from Uncle

Bill how to pick the good from the ones that was too old, also from the poisonous toadstool. The good mushroom is pink underneath, even the small mushroom which is called a "button" and is the best, the older and spoiled mushroom turns dark underneath. The toadstool is always dark underneath, quite a bit darker than the mushroom and the shape of it is thicker and rounder.

While the kids was enjoying themselves at picking mushrooms, Frank untied the bundle from the back of his saddle, and as he unwrapped it out of his slicker by his two riders there come to sight a loaf of bread, some buns, a string of wieners, half a slab of bacon, and two pounds of coffee.

"Doggone if that don't look like a regular picnic spread," says the cowboy, Chuck, as he looked at the food. "I ain't been to a picnic since I was knee-high to what I am now."

"That must of been a long time ago, if a feller was to judge from the length you are now," says Uncle Bill.

There was no trees to get dry limbs from and make a fire, nor no tall brush. The "buffalo chips" was soaked from the last rains and the only thing left was little stunted sage. But there wasn't much fire needed and the sage done well. Wieners was cut open and held over the small but hot fire at a knife's point, so was strips of bacon which was then slipped into the wieners, and all then into a toasted bun.

That went well, so well that even tho Frank had had a good supper in town and wasn't hungry he fixed himself one. Even the kids let up on their mushroom picking long enough to make themselves each a bunful of wiener and bacon. They hadn't been hungry, either, but this wasn't like eating in a restaurant.

"By golly," says Chuck, as he wound up on the fourth bun, "I was just about to talk Bill into butchering one of them two-hundred-dollar pedigreed bulls of yours, Frank, and slice some steaks off of him, but I'll make it now."

"Good thing I come along as I did," grins Frank. "Saved a double slaughter, the bull and you."

The bulls, having their fill, was most all laying down and chewing away at their cud, all content. The few still standing was sniffing the air the direction to where now big dark clouds was piling up on the tail of the thunderheads.

"We made a dry camp," says Uncle Bill. "No water to wash down our victuals, but by the looks of them clouds it won't be dry very long, and I'm thinking them bulls will be more than wanting to travel."

"Yeh," says Frank, "and we better start 'em on trail too and get lined out before it gets too dark. There's no place where we can hold 'em until we get to the corrals at Rock Creek now, and a little bunch like this would be mighty hard to hold in the open. So let's drift."

Wrapping up what was left of the grub, enough for two more meals, it was divided to go into saddle pockets, slickers left free for quick use. The kids was the only ones stuck. There was no pockets on their saddles and being they'd picked near two hatfuls of mushrooms they was kind of up against it as to what to do with 'em. Frank was for telling 'em to leave 'em, that there'd be plenty more, but—

The few still standing was sniffing the air.

"They'll keep good for twenty-four hours," says Scootie, "and by that time we might have a chance to cook 'em."

So there was nothing to do but figuring a way of taking the mushrooms along. "What'd be the matter with putting them in our slicker pockets?" suggests Kip; "slicker pockets are never used anyhow."

In the slicker pockets the mushrooms went, one to two double handfuls to each till all was pocketed away.

"If it rains and the water leaks in my pockets," grins Chuck, "there's liable to be some young mushrooms come to life right while I'm riding."

Flashes of lightning was lighting up the still far away dark clouds, and steady low rumblings of thunder was heard as the cattle was put on the move. They moved well and quick, starting out a bucking and playing, all slick, fine young bulls and full of life.

"Sure enough going to storm all right," says Uncle Bill. "The way they're playing is a good sign."

"Yes," says Frank, "and they'd sure be hard to hold when the storm does come. But we're not going to try to hold 'em, we'll shove 'em right along till we hit Rock Creek."

There was no glorious or gorgeous sunset that evening; the sun went down behind heavy clouds, turning the green range land to dreary gray, then so dark later that hardly no skyline could be seen, like with the cattle which was only a little darker than the land and could not be seen over a few yards away. The riders had to ride close and went pretty well as to where each one was only by the humming of a tune or whistle.

Thunder was heard as the cattle was put on the move.

Then a puff of wind come, stillness, then another puff, till after a while them puffs seemed to've got together and made a steady wind which got stronger and stronger. Frank, seeing the darker shadow of the two kids riding close together, rode near 'em.

"Looks like we're going to get only the edge of this storm," he says, so as to keep the kids from fretting, also hoping he was right and that would be all. "It's good now that the wind is with us, but if things turn to the bad and the cattle get to running and scattering, don't you kids get scared and go to stampeding too, just follow by the sound of the running cattle. You two stick close together and if the bad comes to worse and we all scatter in trying to keep the cattle together and you lose track and sound of us don't be riding around looking for us because on a night like this you'd be sure to get lost. So if we do happen to lose track of one another just get off your horses, squat on your heels inside your slickers and wait till daybreak, that would save yourselves and your horses a lot of unnecessary riding, then at daybreak when you can see you could ride straight south and you couldn't miss Rock Creek. It's the first one you'd come to, and riding up along it you'd come to some corrals on this side of the creek. We'd be camped there. If not you'd better wait."

The wind kept a getting stronger as Frank spoke, and as he turned to advise the kids some more a heavy rain drop splattered on his cheek. That was enough warning, and knowing how quick and thick them drops can come, wetting a man before he can slip his slicker on he heeded the first warning drop, and telling the kids to slip their slickers on he done the same.

"And be sure to put on your coats underneath first," he says. "It might of been hot today but I think you feel it's considerable cooler now, and it'll be doggone chilly thru the night if it rains hard.

"Don't forget what I told you kids now in case the cattle scatter and we get separated in trying to get 'em together, and don't get scared because there's nothing to be scared of."

With that he rode to one side and then the other, seeing as to what sides of the little herd Uncle Bill and Chuck was each riding on, leaving the kids to ride up behind the cattle and very much in the dark, not only in atmosphere and landscape but in their thoughts and a little spooky as to what to expect.

CHAPTER THREE

ⱯLONG FLASH OF LIGHTNING played thru the clouds and lit up the land, and horses and cattle stiffened in their tracks like petrified at seeing their shadow, but with the clap of thunder that followed all come to action as tho they'd been poked in the rump with an electric pointed rod.

But that was just a small first scare and the cattle was easy controlled. They'd also sort of expected the ones following and wouldn't scare so easy. With the first clap of thunder a heavy rain shoved by a strong wind really begin to come and, as Frank had said, would wet a man thru before he could get his slicker untied and half on. The kids was glad to have theirs on in time, and the coat underneath felt good too.

The rain pattered on heavy for a few minutes then let up soon as it had started. More wind, then calm, another flash of lightning, a loud crash of thunder, and then the rain come again, heavier than before and with stinging hail this time. In the thick of it the kids heard a voice. They recognized it as Uncle Bill's but they could hardly see him in the darkness and the old cowboy had to holler loud to be heard thru the storm.

"How goes it, kids?" he hollered at 'em.

"All right," hollered Scootie and "Still here," hollered Kip. The two was glad to hear the old cowboy's voice and have his company, but it wasn't for long, he had to ride on and close to the cattle.

The lightning kept a coming closer and the thunder louder for a spell but the rain had thinned down some, which sort of helped. Then the lightning gradually got to stay up and play in the clouds more, making a near steady light, the thunder quieted to rumblings which got lower and drifting with the lightning which got dimmer, and then dark and quiet again. The storm had passed over.

But there was no break in the heavy clouds, not a star could be seen and a steady drizzle kept up with a stiff breeze. Every buffalo wallow was now running over with the water, deep trails was regular little creeks and every hollow was a lake overflowing to another hollow and on down country.

The cattle and horses splashed and slid on the water-soaked prairie sod. There'd been over three weeks of such weather, with steady rains and heavy showers every day, and the cowboys' wooden stirrups being splashed on steady got wet, stayed wet and went to stretching.

Finally, the skies lit up some to where the kids could see the leaders of the little bunch of cattle, also the riders on each side. The cattle was traveling right along as tho they was anxious to get to the other end. Uncle Bill rode close to the kids who had done well in bringing up the rear.

"Traveling right along, ain't they?" says the old cowboy. "We're over halfways to Rock Creek now, and if they keep this gait up we'll be there about sun-up."

"I wouldn't mind being there right now," says Kip, "and be backing up to a big fire. These straight slickers are not much good for saddle, are they? Anyhow the seat of my saddle is all wet and so is mine, from there on down to my toes."

"Too doggone bad," says Uncle Bill, "but there's some breaks and timber not so far ahead now and at the first likely place I'll build a fire that will dry you two up in no time, even if it rains hard, which I'm afraid is going to happen. I think we're due for another blast and thunderstorm.

"Yes, sir, the storm is coming back on us, looks like we'll have to face it this time, which won't be so easy, but if we can make the Rock Creek rims and breaks we'll at least get shelter and be able to hold the cattle. There'd be no making 'em face a storm like the last one we had, nor holding 'em against it. We'd be taking chances of losing some in this dark and the best and only thing could be done would be to drift with 'em till shelter was found. It was good for us that the last storm was at our back or we'd be anywheres but here. Now I'm thinking that if this same storm comes back on us we better try to reach the breaks quick as we can, because when they come back that way they're usually worse, and we'd have to take it head on this time."

"What makes you think it's coming back?" asks Scootie, a little fretful.

"Well, I'm not so sure it's coming back," says Uncle Bill, "but maybe you've noticed how the lightning and thunder of the storm disappeared and there was no sign of it for a while. Now you'll see some of the lightning again, getting brighter right along. The storm might stay where it is and wear itself out there, but I'm afraid not, I'm afraid it'll come back at us like a boomerang."

"You're not saying this to scare us, are you, Uncle Bill?" asks Kip, not much scared.

"No," joked the old cowboy, "I'm just saying it so you kids won't be getting off your horses and go to picking mushrooms or flowers if the storm comes."

The storm came on but it didn't seem to be coming very fast and all riders was feeling relieved in thinking that they would make the shelter of the breaks before it came. The cattle was going on at good gait and the leaders would of soon been going down into the breaks, when there was a splintering crash as a blinding flash of lightning hit a pine tree at the edge of the breaks and set it to blazing soon as it hit, and to blazing not over fifty feet from where the leaders was, or had been. For at the sudden flash so close, splintering crash and thunder all at once, the cattle just picked up from there and scattered all directions but towards the breaks.

Right about then a sudden heavy rain come, like from turned-over tubs or barrels and for a spell it was all confusion. The riders couldn't see the cattle nor one another and that made it mighty dangerous riding, for a few of them bulls running full speed into a horse and rider sure wouldn't do either any good.

Then the rain let up sharp as it'd come, good sign for another flash of lightning and all eyes was set for a quick look to see by the flash where every rider and cattle was. The flash come, giving a fair chance for a quick glimpse of the goings on. . . . The glimpse showed that the cattle was split in three bunches and

The cattle just picked up from there and
scattered all directions but towards the breaks.

running fanways, but not very far apart as yet. Another flash of lightning showed that two bunches had got pretty well together, but the third bunch was making fast time going back to where it come and there was no turning it.

The thunderstorm blazed away with all it had for over half an hour and gradually soared away to wear itself out on tall and jagged mountain peaks.

But it stayed pitch dark, and when dawn come a couple of hours later it took it a long time to make light on account of the skies being still so heavy with dark soggy clouds, only now it had about stopped raining.

"The worst thunderstorm I ever seen," says Chuck as he throwed another heavy pitch-pine limb on a roaring fire. His only listener was Scootie who was more than enjoying the heat. She'd enjoyed it even more if Kip had been there with her but when come the chance to tally up soon as the storm let up and faint daybreak showed enough light it was found that him and six head of bulls was missing.

Scootie was very much worried as to what might of happened to him. But she wasn't the only one, and the missing of the boy was no more than accounted for when Frank told Uncle Bill and Scootie to hit for the breaks with the rest of the bulls. They'd be easy to drive now and easy to hold once they got 'em in the good sheltered and grassy ravines the breaks was full of. Then a fire could be built and both could warm and dry up. Him and Chuck would go hunt for Kip.

But the old cowboy had reared up at the idea, saying that *he* was out to hunt for Kip, and it would be for either Frank or Chuck to hold the bulls and build the fire for Scootie. So the job fell to Chuck to stay back and he didn't at all kick, for he felt that he could sure stand the sound of a crackling fire and the absorbing of some heat.

On account of the strength of the storm with its driving wind and rain it would be easy enough to tell which way the bulls had run and drifted. They would drift right with it, and it was figured that Kip in trying to hold and turn 'em would be with 'em yet. So, to cover bigger territory at once, they split with the understanding not to get too far apart so that in case one found Kip or the bulls or both he could let the other know and stop him from riding further.

A knoll some few miles away was pointed out as to where each was to meet, and they separated on their own circling way to it. It was anxious and far-seeing eyes that swept over the dreary plain that morning. Every blade of grass was heavy with rain drops and the horses sinking hoof deep at every step. There was quite a few cattle and horses out on that range and it would be impossible to track the bulls thru all the other tracks which was just as fresh. Every bunch of cattle was rode close enough to for sight of the bulls, but what both Uncle Bill and Frank was looking for the most and wanting to see was Kip, on or by his horse and with the bulls. The sight of a rider and the count of the cattle would identify that as him for a long ways.

Uncle Bill was riding along at a slow trot, the fastest gait he dared use on that soggy sod if he didn't want to wear out his horse and be helpless to go on. There wasn't a distant boulder, shape, critter, or horse that he didn't take a second look at, and he was riding over a low rise when he seen four straight and blocky backs, and even at the distance he was he knew for sure that there was four of the bulls he was looking for. He rode closer and his heart turned a queer twist at the sight of them and no Kip. He sort of pictured his horse falling or being turned over on him, being trampled in the mud and all such like which sometimes happens. But after he calmed down a little at the shock, he got to thinking, there was still two bulls to be accounted for, they might of been the leaders and he might be with 'em. These four bulls was good proof that the other two came close to about this same direction.

Getting the lay of the land as to where the bulls was, the old cowboy rode on on his circling way to the knoll where he was to meet Frank. No signs of the two bulls or a single horse track was seen on the way, and as he rode up the knoll, Frank was already waiting there, with not a word of good news or sign.

Uncle Bill then felt sort of cheered that the remaining two bulls hadn't been found, for the finding of 'em without Kip would pretty well mean that there'd been a fall, his horse getting away from him and Kip maybe laying crippled in some hollow. But with the two bulls still missing there was hopes that he'd been with 'em thru the storm, and not being able to turn 'em had just drifted with 'em, as many a cowboy has done with herds,—drifting ahead of blizzards when there's no turning, doing his best to keep the cattle from being pocketed, rimrocked, or jammed up against drift fences to freeze to death. No cowboy ever quits a herd, and Uncle Bill knew that if Kip thought he was riding by the leaders he would never quit 'em either, not if he could help it, and if he was found riding it'd be mighty likely that he'd be with the two bulls, and maybe now bringing 'em back by some other direction.

As the two talked all of that over while steady scrutinizing the country around, Frank got to remembering of what he'd advised the kids before the first storm, to hit straight south if they got separated and lost, south to Rock Creek then up the creek to the corrals.

"Maybe he's with them two bulls and headed that way," says Frank. "If he is we'd be sure to miss him riding this way."

After some figuring, Frank decided it would be the best bet for him to hit cross country to where Kip would be likely to go if he hit south heading for Rock Creek. As for Uncle Bill he decided to go on a little further and then make a bigger circle down country as to where the two missing bulls might of led Kip to in his drifting with 'em thru the storm.

To get a better view of the low rolling prairie Old Bill and Frank stayed on their horses as they talked, and for the last few minutes Uncle Bill's attention had been drawn by what he thought was moving objects, one higher up and as tho it might be a rider. He'd rub his eyes and in the heavy atmosphere and low skies the objects would disappear and then show up again. He got to thinking it was his imagination, for if a person's mind is strong enough in wanting to find anything on the prairie, desert or mountains it can play tricks on him and have him imagine that an object is moving by steady watching it, and, with hoping its what he's after, that object might take that shape. A rock, yucca, or twisted pine can at a long distance be imagined to look like most anything you're most anxious to see. Even oldtimers as Uncle Bill sometimes get fooled that way.

Frank reined his horse to a start, when Uncle Bill stopped him with a motion of the hand.

"Wait a minute, Frank," he says, then he pointed at the dim objects in the distance. "See them specks out there, ain't they moving and don't one of 'em look like a rider?"

Frank squinted and located the objects. "Looks like what you say, all right. Let's see if it is moving."

He got off his horse, took out his six-shooter and wedging it with rocks he sighted it straight for the object and left it be for a short while. In the meantime both of the watchers got to thinking that them objects was getting plainer thru the low hanging misty clouds. Then Frank careful not to touch the gun looked thru the sights and then up at Bill.

"Whatever it is," he says, "it's moved and is to one side of the sights of my gun."

"Are you sure it ain't your gun that slipped?"

"Couldn't," says Frank; "not the way I got it wedged."

"Well, let's ride towards them objects then and make sure," says Uncle Bill. "It ain't much out of where we want to go anyhow."

It was less than a mile to them objects, but thru the foggy atmosphere it was harder to see than five miles on a clear day. One advantage was the shorter distance to cover to find out.

Frank looked thru the sights.

"If it's anything else but Kip and the bulls, by Judas Priest, I'm apt to take a shot at it," says Uncle Bill as him and Frank rode with their eyes glued on the object, which was steady taking shape.

Neither of the riders' hearts was beating very steady as they rode down a swale and where for the time they couldn't see the object or objects, but they'd be pretty close when topping the next low rise and get sight of 'em again. Being anxious they put their horses to a faster gait to the top of the low rise, and—

"By godfrey, Bill, it's—"

"Yep," interrupts Uncle Bill. "It's Kip, him and the two bulls, sure enough."

CHAPTER FOUR

T HERE WAS NO TIME WASTED as Frank and the older cowboy made out the yellow-slickered figure of Kip on his gray horse. Thinking he might be hurt or something, being he was riding so quiet and slow, they rode up to him on a high lope, to be met by a bareheaded grinning face half covered with mud. One whole side of his slicker was mud, as tho he'd wallowed in it, and so was the gray horse, from head to tail.

At the relief of seeing the kid, seeming like all right, the two uncles had to laugh, not from relief only but from the mud-spattered sight of him, hair matted with it, and no hat.

"By golly," says Uncle Bill at the sight of the kid, "it's no wonder I couldn't see him plain before. With that mud all over him and his horse, the same color as the sky and the ground. Even the bulls are pretty well coated with it." Then he asked, "You're not hurt anywheres, are you, Kip?"

"No," says Kip, "only maybe in my shoulder. It feels a little stiff now. My horse slid and fell with me."

"I can easy see that," says Frank, "and it's most likely a strained muscle. But we'll fix that as soon as we get to camp, only about six or eight miles from here. . . . Gee, by the looks of you and your horse you must of been traveling some when he fell, and slid quite a ways."

"My horse slid and fell with me."

"Sure did," says Kip, "and I had to do some fast scrambling to get back in the saddle in time to get out of the way of some of the bulls I heard coming my way."

"Well, and you held the bulls anyway," says Frank.

"Held 'em, nothing. They liked to run me out of the country."

The two bulls Kip had was shoved along to be turned in with the four Uncle Bill had found and all six started for the breaks. All was accounted for now.

After a while of driving behind the six bulls, Uncle Bill, who was watching Kip and noticed him shivering in his saddle, says to Frank:

"Better ride on in with Kip, Frank, and get him to the fire before he catches a heck of a cold or something worse. I'm good and warm and I'll take my time shoving the bulls on in."

"I was just thinking of the same thing, Bill," says Frank, "only for *you* to jog on in with Kip instead of me. It was your idea to come out and locate him in the first place." He grins. "Now you take him on in the rest of the way."

Kip tried to make 'em think he was all right and that there was no need for them to bother with him, but that didn't work, for he looked like he was very much in need of being close to a blazing fire and something hot poured inside of him. So, to save time in arguing about it, Uncle Bill decided to go ahead with Kip.

"Couldn't I find camp alone?" asks Kip, seeing he had to go on.

"No," says Frank, "we don't want to take chances of losing you any more, not right now." Then, to Uncle Bill, he went on, "Chuck's horse will be rested when you get there, so will Chuck, and you tell him to chassay on along the breaks to Morrison's and get a lard bucketful of victuals of the kind we haven't got. We can use the bucket to make some coffee in. We'll graze the cattle on down to Rock Creek this afternoon and he can be by the corrals down there to meet us."

With that, which Uncle Bill thought was a mighty good idea, him and Kip started jogging on ahead, leaving Frank to poke with the now slow moving bulls. They'd had their run.

"Looks like there's going to be some more rain," says Uncle Bill, as him and Kip rode on at a good blood circulating jog, "but I don't think it'll be any more wild thunderstorm like we had last night, too daggone cold, and if it rains I don't think it'll be until tonight either. By that time we'll have a shelter built and a rip-snorting fire going, and some hot coffee down our gizzards. Does that sound all right to you?" he asks.

"Sure does," says Kip, grinning at the old cowboy. Then he asked, "How is sis, Scootie? Is she all right?"

"You bet she is. Right by a big fire that Chuck built and which you're going to warm your own self by soon."

They come to the edge of the breaks, and looking back in the distance they could see Frank coming along with the bulls. He was making fair time. Then they come to the pine tree the lightning had struck the night before. Being mostly pitch it had burned down till there was nothing left but a charred, hollowed trunk. The deep tracks of where the cattle had stopped and then turned so sudden in their stampede was mighty close to the burned tree and made so deep that the heavy rains that followed hadn't washed 'em out, only filled 'em full.

It was good to ride off the bleak and dreary prairie down into the breaks. The rough shelter of 'em—wind-hewed caves in the tall rimrocks, pine, cedar and quaker trees and little grassy hollows here and there—all made it like a cheerful and cozy welcome home after the experiences of the night before.

A couple of miles of winding ravines and washes and then the main bunch of the bulls was seen, some still grazing but the most of 'em laying down and chewing their cud in content. They'd had plenty of water and grass. But what Kip was interested in the most right then was the sight of the fire as they come around the point of a rim, and Scootie and Chuck looking so comfortable and warm right there.

There was happy grins as all met again, specially from Scootie as she seen her mud-covered brother. As tired and cold as Kip was he first took care of his little gray before coming to the fire. Refusing any help, he took the saddle and bridle off and only hobbled him, a little stream of rain water was still running in the grassy hollow.

At the fire, Kip took his slicker and shaps off so the heat would get to him quick, and then, turning one side and the other to it, is when he really begin to smile.

Uncle Bill took on some of the heat himself, then speaking to Chuck who was also by the fire, he asks:

"Did you have any rest while we was gone?"

"Some," says Chuck, "enough, and something to eat too. Miss Scootie and me took turns about watching the cattle but they was no trouble at all and neither of us had to get on our horses over a couple of times."

Uncle Bill took on some of the heat himself.

"Well," says Uncle Bill, "there's a little job that Frank would like to have you do," and he told Chuck about his riding to the Morrisons' and so on. "Get to riding, cowboy, and never mind visiting too long with Julie Morrison this time," the old cowboy grinned. "She'll keep."

Chuck grinned back as he buttoned his coat and pulled up his shaps. "Sure she'll keep," he says, "but you know how it is about spring and when a young man's fancy turns to thoughts of, and so on. . . . Well, anyway I'll be by the corrals on Rock Creek and have a big fire going when you all get there with the bulls."

With that he went to where his saddled horse had been grazing close by, took the hobbles off of him, and getting in the saddle waved a "so long" and rode away.

"Good hand, that boy," says Uncle Bill as he watched him ride away. "Good man in every way."

Then turning to the kids: "Well, what do you say we throw a bait? I'm hungry enough to eat mutton."

"I could eat mutton myself," says Kip, "or most anything. Can I be of any help?"

"Yes, you can stay right where you are, get dry and warm up."

Then Scootie spoke up. "I don't care for any more to eat right now," she says, "so I'll take your place at watching the cattle. I had plenty of rest and sleep to do me for a while too, which is more than either of you had."

So Uncle Bill went to work looking thru what was left of the grub that'd been packed on the saddles and all left on a slab of rock. There was still plenty of bacon, a few wieners and buns and bread. The bread had got well soaked up and then being dried by the fire had got good and hard, but it was bread, and hunks of it toasted by the fire with strips of bacon and a roasted wiener or two didn't go at all bad. Doggone good, thought Kip. After they had their fill, which revived the two a considerable, there was still plenty left for Frank when he'd ride in, and more too.

There was no need of gathering wood, for Chuck had taken care of that. Big limbs was burned in two, the ends throwed on the fire afterwards, and being there was nothing for the old cowboy to do for the time being excepting to watch over the kids and see that none of the cattle got away he thought strong of taking a short nap. And with Scootie saying that she'd be glad to watch over the cattle for something to do, letting him know if anything went wrong, and Kip now leaning back, warmed up and about asleep, that all was a mighty good opening for him to at least stretch out for a while. He did that, and in a few minutes he was asleep.

When he woke and sat up the sky was still clouded but much lighter. Must of slept quite a while, he thought because it looked like high noon. If so, Frank should of been back long before now. He rubbed his eyes and, looking towards the cattle first, thought he spotted Frank's rangy bay grazing this side of 'em, then looking by Kip there was Frank, sound asleep beside the boy. He noticed too as he looked at the flat rock that more of the grub had been used. Uncle Bill grinned. Must of been awful quiet or I must of been awful tired, he thought, or I'd sure woke up.

Kip was still asleep. Then wondering about Scootie he was glad to see her riding back towards the fire. All was well. So, quiet as he could be he piled some more limbs on the fire, squatted by it and rolled a smoke, all content.

As Uncle Bill figured it was near middle afternoon when Kip finally stirred and woke up. With that, Frank woke up, seeming like pretty well rested and ready for another hard ride. A cowboy can sleep long in a short time.

"Well, I guess I needed that sleep," says Frank, rubbing his eyes.

"Sure," says Uncle Bill who, standing by Scootie, had just got back from a look-see at the cattle, "and with some good hot coffee down you and Kip, you'll both feel as pert as a couple of chipmunks."

At the sound of coffee and as tho Uncle Bill meant it, Frank looked acrost the fire at the old cowboy. "I suppose if a man was starving to death," he says, grinning, "you'd add on to his torture by mentioning roast beef and browned potatoes."

"I'm not joking," says Uncle Bill. "I have got some real strong and hot coffee for yez. If you think I'm joking just stand on your legs and follow me a ways."

Frank knowing that the old cowboy wasn't up to any such fool tricks as to make a man walk, even only a few yards, to play a joke on him at such a time, got up and told Kip to come along. "But I'm from Missouri," he says, "and you got to show me."

"Well, I'm from Texas," says Uncle Bill, "and I can show you."

Away from the fire about a hundred yards they come to where steam could be seen coming out of a hollowed place in a big sand rock by the tall rim. Before getting to it, Uncle Bill nudged Frank's elbow, winked at him and for Kip's benefit, he says:

"Yes, it's a natural coffee spring I just located. Never was so surprised in my life, and I wouldn't believed it, only I seen the steam, smelled of it, tasted it and by gollies it was coffee. I drank a lot of it. Scootie did too."

Frank, still a mite dubious, didn't give up till he come to the hollowed hole in the rock and smelled. Then seeing what had been done he squinted at the old cowboy and with a crooked grin he says:

"Bill, you're a wizard—Moses had nothing on you when he tapped the side of a dry mountain with a little stick and started a spring trickling down the sides of it."

"Too bad that coffee spring don't throw in a little cream and sugar, but you can drink coffee black, can't you? It'll sure warm you up inside."

Squashing his hat so the brim would sort of cup and do to drink out of, Uncle Bill dipped it in the coffee hollow and handed it to Kip who, a little unbelieving, took and begin to drink. It was hot and strong, and he made faces, but it was good, and to his surprise it was sure enough coffee. He'd tasted black coffee before.

Frank didn't have no more remarks to pass as he dipped his hat brim time and again for more of the coffee, smacking his lips and puffing at a cigarette between swallows. The coffee left stains on the hat brims, but none cared about that, for coffee was the most important just then. The cowboy seldom wears or has anything that won't stand his use, the sun, wind and rain would soon enough take the stain away, and being of good stuff it will stand other uses.

Scootie'd had her fill. So did Uncle Bill while Frank and Kip had been sleeping, and now seeing that the "coffee spring" was about to run dry, Kip mentioned the fact.

"Yes," says Uncle Bill, winking at Frank, "it runs pretty slow. I'll see what I can do about it."

Taking Scootie along, he started back for the fire, while Scootie went above it to where the rain water had dammed up and cleared.

He dipped his hat brim time and again for more of the coffee.

In a short while they both came back, Uncle Bill with a green willow basket he'd weaved to carry heated round rocks in, and Scootie with her hat crown full of water which carried near a gallon.

In the "coffee spring," Scootie emptied her hatful of water, Uncle Bill added more coffee grounds and then the hot rocks was eased in one at a time, setting the water to bubbling and steaming right away. A slicker was then placed over the hollow to hold down the steam, and fresh coffee was soon ready.

"You'd got along good in the cave man days," grins Frank.

"But," says Kip looking a little ashamed at being fooled, "this is not a spring. I can see that now. I know how the water is heated and the coffee is made, but would you tell me about the hole in the rock? I know you didn't make that."

"No," grins Uncle Bill, "old man weather and time made that with the start of a few wind blown gravels. It took hundreds of years, but with the winds blowing up a few gravels to where they caught hold and was whirled around with more coarse gravel accumulating, then years after years of more winds and ice and snow, heavy rains and hail like last night, with the winds steady whirling the gravels around and around, wore a cavity to the size you see now. In a few more hundred years it'll be the size of a washtub, till with time this big rock crumbles to pieces."

Uncle Bill pointed at caves and holes alongside the rims: "Them's made the same way, by winds and sands and rushing waters, and if you'll look you'll see more rocks with holes in 'em just like this. In the summer time when it's dry, like in the desert, horses and cattle will hunt up these kind of holes after a rain and do well on 'em until they dry up and thirst drives the stock back to the main watering places."

"And getting back to the coffee," says Frank, "now that we have some fresh, what do you all say we eat what's left and start on down country with the cattle. They act like they want to drift."

That was all right by all, and now, being that the hot coffee couldn't be packed to the fire what was left of the grub was packed to the coffee, and there the four went on to finish all. The hard bread was "dunked," as Scootie called it, into the coffee and all done the same till the last crumb was gone. Everything was et up but the bacon rind when they got thru, and that was left for the chipmunks.

"I hope Chuck's horse don't fall off the side of a rim, or anything happens so as to keep him from getting to the corral with the grub," says Frank, while all was tying their slickers back on their saddles and getting ready to move. "If he don't get there it'll be just a fire and up a couple of holes in the belt for us."

"You're a cheerful cuss," snorts Uncle Bill. "Never heard you talk that way before. You know doggone well Chuck will make it. Besides it wouldn't be the first time you missed quite a few meals at a stretch while doing some hard riding and I never heard you mention it before."

"I wasn't thinking of us old rawhide-bellies, Bill," he says. "It's the kids."

"Yeh, that's right," says Uncle Bill, serious. Then he grinned a little. "But we still have some coffee."

Overhearing that last remark, Scootie came up smiling and saying, "And we also have some mushrooms."

The whole outfit had to smirk at that, then Frank says, "We'll see if we can't get something on the way to go with 'em."

The cattle was shoved together and, all accounted for, was started down country towards Rock Creek, and having had their fill of grass and water and being rested they traveled well. It was figured that even with taking 'em slow and grazing 'em along, the corral would be reached in about four hours, and it would still be daylight.

Some grouse and sage hens was seen once in a while amongst the sage and cedars, also some deer which run only a short ways only to stop, turn broadside and stare with them big eyes of theirs. Fine targets for hunters, and either Frank or Uncle Bill could of got one of 'em with their six-shooters, if they wished.

But a cowboy is seldom much for shooting anything down unless the meat is needed. A good young sage chicken would be just about right now, thought Frank, and if they kept on showing themselves he'd try and get one. They kept on showing themselves, and his chance come as he was riding at the edge of the cattle and along the side of a brush-covered hill, when quite a few sage chickens come to his sight. Some of 'em looked near as heavy as a big tame duck and so fat they waddled around in about the same way, trying very little to hide, and none showed signs of wanting to fly as Frank rode to within fifty feet of 'em and got off his horse. Being there was no slaughtering hunters from towns ever come to that country they was very tame, and Frank, not wanting to scare 'em, didn't draw his gun to get his meat. Instead he just picked up a few likely rocks and come a little closer to the chickens, which only raised their heads at him and slowly walked on.

He picked out what he thought was a young rooster, let a rock fly at him, and missed, but the chickens still just walked on. Frank walked a little faster, and with his third rock he seen his chicken flounder around with one wing dragging and hitting for a bush to hide in. It was easy to pick up then and the others only walked faster to keep away as he did, none flew.

"Well," says Frank to the kids after he'd tied the chicken to his saddle and got on his horse, "now we have chicken to go with the mushrooms and coffee."

It begin to get warmer as the afternoon wore on and then lighter as tho the sun would come out, but no sun, and later on it seemed to've got lighter only like to make room for heavy dark clouds which come a rolling to replace the spent ones of the night before. Then after a while, low and far away rumblings of thunder begin to be heard again, and faint showing of lightning. The cattle raised their heads and sniffed at the air.

"Looks like we're due for another wetting," says Uncle Bill, just watching the cattle. "Them bullocks act kind of nervous."

"Let 'er come, bust and flicker," says Frank. "We'll be in camp and shelter before it hits us, and there won't be no driving or holding of them bullocks tonight. We'll let 'em graze on till dark and then slam 'em in the corral. That'll be easier on both man and beast."

Mile after mile of muddy tracks was left behind as the cattle wound their way thru the breaks, still going slow and grazing along, and then when the dark clouds, like heavy-loaded with dynamite, seemed to come faster than was figured they would, Frank gave word to crowd the cattle on in.

"They can graze some more when we get there," he says, "but we got to hustle on now if we're going to make some kind of shelter before this skyful of thunderbolts hits us and washes us away. Goshamighty, I hope Chuck got back."

Another couple of miles and finally around the point of a ridge come the sight of the tall cottonwood groves bordering Rock Creek, and then come a big surprise, for Rock Creek wasn't a creek no more. The rains had swelled it till it got above the banks a few feet deep, run wild, and spread thru the cottonwood groves and bottoms.

"Well, I'll be a cross-eyed, knock-kneed monkey," says Frank all at once as he sized up the spread of the creek. "Why, we're lost. This ain't Rock Creek; looks more like the Missouri River to me."

There was a rush now to see if the water had got as high as the corrals. If so that would mean standing guard on the cattle that night. But as good luck would have it, or as the far-seeing old timer who'd built the corral had thought of such as floods and cloudbursts the corral was still far from reach of the rushing wild waters.

Then come another surprise, a different kind of a one, for by the spring above the corral was a tent and looked like a whole camping outfit. Two horses was hobbled and grazing a ways from it.

"Looks like we have visitors," says Uncle Bill.

"Or that they're going to have visitors, you mean," says Frank.

The cattle was dropped on a grassy spot where they could be watched from the camp, and the four rode on up. There to see a tarp stretched as a lean-to and a tepee tent to one side. Wood had been gathered and by it was a frying pan and a kettle.

Seeing nobody around, Frank was about to holler for whoever might be near when Uncle Bill, whose curiosity had got the best of him, opened the little tent's flap and then whistled low at Frank to come look. Frank did and there, stretched out and sound asleep on a tarpaulin covered round-up bed, was Chuck.

"Well, I'll be—," was all Frank could say.

CHAPTER FIVE

HERE WAS NO TIME FOR TALK. The heavy clouds were rolling on, noisy and mighty threatening, and the lean-to and tent was tied down some more to make sure of holding against the strong winds and driving rains that was sure to come. Kip and Scootie and Uncle Bill "snaked" down more dry limbs and dead trees from the side of the hills and piled 'em up on the already big pile which Chuck had stacked there.

"Must be figuring on staying all summer," says that cowboy as he was hammering at a peg with a rock.

"Well, it'll come in handy," says the old cowboy. "Not only for us but for the others who'll come afterwards."

The camp well set, the six-thousand-dollar herd, as Chuck called the bunch of bulls, had to be put to other grass and more shelter before the coming storm struck. There was a little discussing as to who was going to take 'em, but Uncle Bill, with the help of the two kids finally won, saying they'd take 'em.

Right around the point from where they'd come was a brushy canyon boxed in by rimrock and there's where the bulls was drove into, less than half a mile from camp. At the mouth of the canyon and at the foot of the rim was a cave deep enough for good shelter. The cattle could be well watched from there, but there was no fear of any trouble with 'em, for cattle scattered, in good feed and shelter the way them was, are not likely to scare and stampede like cattle being held close together in the open, or driven.

The three brought in some dry limbs broken from standing trees and started a fire inside the cave. They'd be there only for a couple of hours, maybe till dark, but it had turned cool and there's nothing like a blazing fire to cheer things when it rains. Heavy drops was already beginning to fall, and what more would be coming didn't need to be guessed at.

But the three in the cave would be comfortable and well out of reach of wind and rain. Their horses was tied in a sheltered place and to low cedars, not pine, because pine or any evergreen draws lightning more than other trees. The slickers was spread over the saddles and tied, not only to keep the saddles dry but also the horse as much as possible.

Like as tho the storm had waited till all was set, to sort of make up for the grief it had given the night before, it then broke loose sudden, wild and furious. Lightning was hitting all directions, trees could be heard crashing and rolling down the steep hillsides and off rims. It came so heavy for a time that a few feet was about the furthest the three could see outside of their cave, and if the cattle came past and out of the canyon there'd been no way of knowing at the time. But nothing could of been done about it, for cattle couldn't be held nor turned in that storm, they couldn't of been seen nor the cattle see the riders. But in the good shelter they was in, Uncle Bill figured they'd stay well.

The lightning and thunder stopped but the rain came on and like in barrelsful all being dumped at once. "By gollies,

The three in the cave would be comfortable.

children," says Uncle Bill, "this ain't no heavy rain nor shower, it's a regular old time cloudburst of the kind I haven't seen for years. God help some of them ranches on down Rock Creek, specially after the heavy rains of last night. I know of some of them down there that's sure going to get flooded and washed out. Not high enough from the creek.

"As far as we're concerned," the old cowboy went on, "it looks like we'll have to stay at our camp by the corral for a couple of days and till the creek goes down so we can cross without taking chances of losing any of the bulls. But the waiting won't be hard to take if it clears up a little so we can dry our hides."

As with most cloudbursts or heavy showers it stopped near as quick as it started. With this one it seemed to've cleaned the skies of all other clouds and film as it went, headed east, and like a thick black curtain, lifted in time to reveal the setting sun to shine on the water-soaked range.

Standing at the edge of their cave with the fire at their back and facing the sun's rays the three felt their spirits rise to near equal of the great sight before 'em. There was no equal to that sight. It was beyond describing or even fully feeling. It just made a person want to take it in with deep breaths and not say a word.

The last rays of the sun had gone when Kip broke the quiet. "Gee," he says, "I wish that good old sun was coming up instead of going down. I could stand a whole day of it, and a few blisters to boot."

"I could stand some of it myself," says Uncle Bill, "and most likely it'll shine on us tomorrow."

As he spoke he looked down the gully for the bulls. He seen a few here and there coming out of the brush and shelter, and he felt that all would be there, for if one went they most likely all would. It was now time to get 'em together and start 'em for the corral. It would be just about dark by the time they'd get there. So, getting down from their cave thru the brush they was soon to their horses, slickers tied back, and into their saddles again.

When they turned the point of the ridge with the cattle and got sight of the corral they also got sight of a bright fire soaring high and lighting up the camp there.

"I'll bet my top hat that fire was nothing but steaming coals after the cloudburst hit it," grins Uncle Bill.

And he was right. The bulls was corralled, the gate tied shut, and as the three was unsaddling and hobbling their horses near camp they was informed in a joking way by Chuck that the fire had been built fresh, and especially for them.

"Well," Scootie comes back at him, "that's good. We had a fire too but it didn't go out during the storm like yours did. We had ours in a nice cave."

"Yes," Chuck went on, "but you had to come home to the main camp to eat, didn't you? And if you don't believe we have it, just let your peepers roam over this and then tell me you're not hungry."

At that he raised a cloth off some loin steaks that'd just been cut from the main hunk. "These are to go on the coals," he says. Then he raised a tin plate to show a big panful of potatoes already started to fry. "But here," he says, "here's your dish, Scootie." And he raised the lid off the kettle to show her the mushrooms a boiling in good shape. Then there was coffee in the lard bucket, and pan bread just made. "And that ain't all," says Chuck. Unwrapping a round package, he says, "It's a little squashed from being in the pack but you can tell what it was, and it's still good." It was a good sized hunk of fruit cake.

Well, there was no doubt but what there'd be a mighty good feed that night, with plenty of time to eat it in and a good clear starry sky to eat it under. There was no set table of fancy dishes, silverware on lacy tablecloths or such. For plates there was just flat stones brushed and cleaned with rain dripping leaves. Fingers and teeth done for forks and knives, and what lacked in style was more than made up with clean appetites and open air. Night birds of all kinds, with hoot owls as timers, went to make up the orchestra.

Frank and Chuck was the chief cooks, and leaving them at their job, Uncle Bill and the kids went to wash where the water was running over a little dam below the spring and near the camp. When they got back they all picked their places where they laid their stone plates, and then each went to cooking their own steaks, over coals or blaze, whichever way they liked. The rest of the food was all ready and the feast was soon at full swing.

"Looks to me like," says Uncle Bill to Chuck, "that you must of robbed two or three camps to get all this grub, and such."

"Now," Chuck says turning to Frank who was sitting near him. "Now, there's gratitude for you." The cowboy acted hurt. "The old scalawag ought to be durn thankful to get such a spread without passing any such accusing remarks."

Uncle Bill grinned in his whiskers. "Julie still must think a lot of you," he went on, for another dig at Chuck, "and her mammy and pappy must of been gone for her to let you get away with all this."

"Hang on to me, Frank," says Chuck, "before I do damage and throw all my 'dishes' at what this talk is coming from."

After a while he went on, like trying to prove himself innocent from a crime. "Here," he says, "you gentlemen put yourself in my place. . . . I rides up to the Morrison ranch, and what do you suppose I runs up to first?"

"The gate, of course," says Uncle Bill."

"No. The gate was open. It was the pup. Well, the pup barks, and now comes Julie on the scene, I mean on the porch. Her mother comes to the door, and the squeak of the corral gate down below lets me know that Dad Morrison is coming up."

"Well, as you all know," Chuck went on, more serious, "it was my intentions of getting only a little dab of stuff, just what I could easy enough take on my saddle without making my horse bow-legged, but I come there just a little while before dinner and by the time I got thru explaining our fix the table was set and nothing would do but what I had to pull a chair up to it."

Uncle Bill seen an opening. "I suppose that hurt," he says.

"Well," grins Chuck, "I was sitting by Julie, so you can kind of imagine. . . . Anyhow." He went on, "I was kind of telling the old folks about us getting caught in the storm while we et, how nice it was, running out of chuck and so on. Then I happened to mention the kids here in saying how many of us there was, and at that Mrs. Morrison and Julie liked to spilled their coffee, and Mrs. Morrison says, 'Why the poor children,' and when she asked how they was and I had to admit they'd got a little chilled, why that sort of shortened the meal some.

"The ladies went one way and Pop another, and with me running back and forth a trying to say that they shouldn't go to no fuss, that we didn't need this nor that, couldn't pack it on my saddle and so on I was getting pretty leg-weary and winded. Finally, it relieved and surprised me both when Pop said for me not to worry about taking the stuff, that he'd let me have a good pack horse, and as you see what I brought it did take a good pack horse. Pop went to the store room and drug out his round-up bed first thing, throwed a slab of bacon and a hunk of beef in a flour sack and wrapped it in this tarp I've got stretched for shelter, then he drug out the tepee, and said it was for the kids.

"I tried to say a few words that there was no need for all the stuff, but you know the Morrisons. To get me out of the way, Pop told me to hit for the corrals and catch a big black horse out of a bunch, the only black in there, and cinch the pack saddle on him, and bring the 'paniers' too. . . . Well, sir, by the time I led the black up to the porch, I sized that horse up again and was glad to see that he was plenty big and strong and had good legs under him, for what with all the ladies had brought on the porch to be put in the paniers and then what Pop had by the store house to put on top and wind up the pack I figured I would need two pack horses. But the black was near big enough for two and I was thankful for that.

"I had a heck of a time a trying to make the ladies keep back some of the stuff but didn't have much luck. Finally the pack was tied to stay and I led the black away before anything else could

The black was near big enough for two and I was thankful for that.

be fastened on him. And here I am," says Chuck as a windup; "done my good deed, near sweated blood to have grub and a good comfortable camp ready for you all, and here I get accused by a bewiskered old magpie of being a camp robber."

Frank and the kids eyes Uncle Bill like to shame him for persecuting such a good and innocent man as Chuck, but all they could get out of him was wrinkles of a grin around his eyes as he looked down at his stone "platter" and went on eating.

Quite a bit of conversing went around the big crackling and cheerful fire that evening. About the swelling of the creek to a big wild river, what damage it would do with some of the ranches in the lower country, along with the good it would do to the range. There was stories told of this and that flood in different years, and what damage and good they'd done, and all thru the talk the kids listened well, for they'd just had a good taste of heavy rains, wicked lightning and thunder, all capped by a real cloudburst, and now there was the flood.

"Good thing," Frank was saying, "that we have enough grub to do us for a day or two and till the creek goes down so we can cross it without taking chances of losing any of the bulls. This creek crossing is pretty bad, the banks on both sides being so steep. Any stock carried down stream by swift waters and the other side of the crossing being missed there'd be a dangerous swim of about a mile before any could get out, and they'd most likely drown along the way.

"There was a cowboy drowned here at this same crossing only last year. It was after a heavy shower, not a cloudburst, but the creek had raised quite a few feet and was running swift. This cowboy, Lou Shay was his name. I don't think you fellers got to know him. Anyhow he was leading a half-broken bronc, and nobody really ever got to know how it happened but it was figured the bronc jerked back in the middle of the stream and turned the saddle horse and rider over backwards, and down the stream they all went, missing the other side of the crossing.

"The horses was found down the creek about a mile caught in the roots of a washed down tree. The lead rope from the bronc's head with the end tied fast to the saddle horn on the other horse is what had held 'em there to soon drown. The cowboy was found about a month afterwards, buried in a little washed up mud island in the middle of the creek. Only the spurred heels of his boots and part of his shaps was showing.

"Yes, sir," Frank went on, "that's a dangerous crossing when the creek is high and I figure that an extra day of waiting is mighty cheap and not to be compared to a life, even if it might be only an animal's." Frank was thinking mostly of the kids' safety.

"If I'd had an idea we was going to bump into this kind of weather and have *company* with us," he grinned at the kids, "and then be held up here by the creek I'd had the chuck wagon, loaded with bed rolls and grub, come along. But not expecting anything like this I depended on my car coming along to get Kip and Scootie

Only the spurred heels of his boots and part of his shaps was showing.

and bring us grub at the same time. But no automobile could budge out of the ranch in the weather we've had, the first gumbo hill or little wash crossing would be where the car would stay until dry weather, or four good horses come to pull it out. So I don't think the car was even started from the ranch. They'd think we stayed in town and held the bulls in the railroad pen overnight."

He looked at Kip and Scootie, and asked: "Don't you wish we had, now?"

There was the sideways shake of two heads, and the same answer that followed left no doubt but what they'd go thru the same storm again rather than stay in town any short length of time.

CHAPTER SIX

KIP THOUGHT IT WAS CLOUDY when morning come and he first blinked his eyes above, but it was the canvas of the little tepee he was in, and as he woke up more he begin looking around to sort of get his bearings. He remembered the round-up bed, of the men taking a few "soogans" out of it to roll up in under the canvas shelter by the fire. He remembered of taking only his coat and boots off, the same as Scootie had and of their both rolling under a tarp'-covered quilt. Then he didn't remember no more.

He looked at Scootie, she was still dead to the world. No sound come to his ears from outside excepting that of the distant rushing waters and the chirping of birds. All being so quiet he figured the men to've gone somewhere, or maybe still asleep. He'd had plenty of sleep himself, seemed like the best he'd had for months, and he had enough now. He slipped on his boots then his coat and came out of the tent, and thinking it was barely sun-up on account of the night going by so fast he was surprised as he blinked at a bright and warming sun, quite a few hours high in the sky.

But it was no surprise to him then that nobody was around, and he wondered where they could all have gone to. He looked down to the corral and seen that the bulls had been let out to

*He was surprised as he blinked at a warm and brightening sun,
quite a few hours high in the sky.*

graze, or at least they wasn't in there. Then looking towards the grazing horses he noticed that his Uncle Frank's and Chuck's horses was missing, but he seen that both his and Scootie's was there, also Uncle Bill's and the borrowed black, so, according to the horses left, Uncle Bill should be around somewhere, and he couldn't of been gone long because the fire was still blazing good.

Well, he'd fix himself up some breakfast, and while he'd be cooking or eating it somebody would most likely show up. He thought of getting Scootie up but thought again that it would be best to let her sleep. It was good to be alone for a change anyway. He'd often dreamed of just this while at home or school in the East, of being alone in the rough hills, at his camp and his horse grazing not far away in the bright sun. Now that was all before him as he'd visioned it many times before in the printed pages of his school books. He would play "Sourdough" and drifting cowboy, looking at the blue ridges wondering where to hit for next and all such like that goes with the life.

But first, before going on any make-believe wild adventure, he'd have to mix and cook himself a bait. He'd pretty well forgot from the summer before just how to make biscuits or flapjacks, but that would soon come to him again. In the meantime, and while rummaging around, he noticed the frying pan upside down on a rock by the fire, like it was covering something, and it was. As he lifted it there come to sight a good batch of pancakes with strips of bacon laid acrost 'em. On the warm rock by the fire and covered by the frying pan they'd kept near as good as tho fresh cooked. Then on some coals, also close to the fire, was the coffee, steaming hot.

Well, that put Kip out as to cooking his own breakfast, and it was just as well because there was no oversupply of flour and such, and Kip's first few batches might of not turned out so good. But these pancakes on the warm rock, a strip of bacon rolled inside of one, was good. So was the coffee, even tho without cream or sugar, and when Kip got thru he didn't at all feel disappointed that he didn't get to cook his own breakfast.

Seeing that all was already straightened up in camp and nothing to do there he walked down to the corral, there to see if the bulls had broke out during the night or if they'd been turned out. The gate well opened and wide showed they'd been left out and to graze. Then looking towards the still swollen and rushing waters he seen that it had gone down considerable during the night. Uprooted trees and dead timber was piled high and deep on the creek banks, but more was still a coming and rushing down country.

As Kip watched the wild waters from the corral he thought he seen house logs float by, then pieces of lumber and some home or camp belongings, and he figured that if the flood got to sweeping what few scattering places was up along the creek it would sure do plenty of damage on down further, where there was more and bigger ranches and the creek wider.

When he would build his ranch, he thought, he would make sure that it'd be in some high location and safe from any flood, at least as high from any creek or river as the corral he was now sitting by. This was one lesson he'd learned and which the settlers on the creek should of also thought of, but as Frank had said there'd never been any such cloudbursts or floods in that country, none that he'd ever heard of and none that he himself had seen in the forty-five years of his life.

"But I guess this one will be remembered," Chuck had said to that.

Kip's thoughts and watching of the waters was interrupted by a holler from up the camp, and he turned to see Scootie waving at him. His lone cowboy days was over for the time being.

Getting up to camp he helped his sister find the same things he'd had for breakfast, and as she settled down to eat Uncle Bill walked in on the two.

"Well, it looks like all is accounted for," he says as a good morning greeting. "I just been up the side of the hill doing a little hunting."

He was carrying two sage chickens and laid 'em on a rock.

"Good, hot or cold," he grinned, "or even raw when you're hungry enough." Then he asked, "How's my patients this morning? You both look chirp."

And they both felt that way, they said.

After some little conversation, Uncle Bill picked up an old broken-handled shovel which had been found by the corral and begin digging a small pit not far from the fire. That done he scraped some coals in it and piled on some wood to make more coals and heat the pit, as an oven. While the fire was burning he took the two chickens, also the one Frank had got the day before and went up to the spring with 'em, where he cleaned the insides out and washed 'em, then at camp he mixed a thick batter and with sliced potatoes and bacon that went for the stuffing.

That done and the feathers being left on the chickens for such purpose, he made a sticky paste of clay and molded it, covering each chicken with a good thickness of it. The clay stuck good to the wet feathers and when each chicken was well plastered that way they looked like a big football.

The fire had burned down to a good layer of coals by the time the chickens was ready. A space was made where each was laid with the coals under and between, more of the live coals from the open fire was piled thick on top and then the whole thing was covered with earth till it made a small mound.

"Well, now," says Uncle Bill, as he called his work done, "there's no more to that until it's time to eat supper. They'll be well done and tender by then."

The kids didn't miss one move the old cowboy had made while fixing the chickens. They followed him from the pit to the spring and back again, watched him stuff 'em, roll 'em in clay and cover 'em up with coals and earth, and now they was sure they could prepare and cook chickens in the same way.

Any plain hunk of meat could be cooked in that way too, Uncle Bill had told 'em. . . . Just wrap the meat in a clean cloth first, then cover it with a gunny sack. The sack would be for the clay or mud to stick to, the same as it did with the chicken feathers, and the inside cloth would be to keep the meat clean. If onions can be had, cut slits in the meat, press some slices into the slits, salt and pepper well, and when all that is cooked in together, none of the good getting out, and the baked clay shell is broke open there lays a hunk of meat no chef or meat eater can begin to sneeze at. Some time the kids would sure try to cook that way.

The rest of the forenoon was spent in the drying of clothes and such which still held some of the moisture of the storm, and being the day was clear and the sun shined bright and warm the kids stripped down to their underwear and overalls, went barefooted and got full benefit of the sun's drying rays. Kip's shoulder wasn't bothering him much now and he seldom was reminded of it unless he laid on it or moved too quick. That would soon wear off, Uncle Bill had said, and when they'd get to the ranch, Martha would sure see to that.

The sun was nearing high noon when Chuck, who'd been graze-herding the bulls, rode up to camp. He'd left the bunch where they wouldn't be apt to stray away during the heat of the day and he felt safe in taking his time to visit at the camp a while. No cowboy ever likes to herd, too slow a work, not enough doing and is just plain monotonous. With the workings of good outfits the cowboy is mighty thankful there's very little of that to do.

"I expect it's time to eat again," says Uncle Bill, as Chuck came into camp. "Whoever put the monicker of Chuck onto you was sure of picking one that didn't chafe, and that whoever it was didn't have to be much of a hand at knowing human nature either because chuck is wrote all over your face, and if that monicker is ever changed I'm sure it'll be Grub."

Chuck didn't say anything at the remarks for a spell. He just grinned with the kids who grinned back at him and then went to investigating as to what'd been done towards starting a noon bait. Finally, as Uncle Bill kept a harping and got to digging a little deeper on account of getting no response, Chuck came to the front to try and save his name from more mistreating. A cowboy's great pleasure is a good battle of wits whenever there comes a chance, and a good laughing joke that the other feller can't get out from under with some good comeback is something worth battling for. It might be some time before the loser can think up a good comeback but he'll seldom give up.

Chuck, like with most cowboys, wasn't a very heavy eater, not as compared with the average man of other trades who also work out of doors. But Uncle Bill thinking of no other subject at the time to start a fast-going conversation with, natural like stumbled on the grub subject.

"There's one thing about grub or chuck or whatever you may want to call food," says Chuck as he rolled a smoke and squinted at the skillet, "it's always cheerful to think of. It's not only good for the mind and heart but it eases the innard pains and makes a feller content. Grub or chuck is pleasing to the ear and nose when meat and potatoes is a frying or coffee is a boiling. If you're not within hearing or smelling distance the eye gets it and lingers in the mind, and even if it ain't there imagination even goes to work and makes you vision baits that makes your mouth water. . . . No, sir, I don't see nothing wrong with the sound or the use of chuck or grub unless it's to be old crabby dyspeptics who're soured on everything they look at, why chuck and grub are not words to be mentioned. Such kind are more happy to hurt their toe at kicking a rock or roll in a cactus bed than they would sitting with a hunk of pie in the shade of a peach tree and listening to a babbling brook."

Seeing that his subject didn't have enough strength to pack him thru without making it long-winded, Uncle Bill sort of chopped it off by saying:

"Well, if you're so all fired strong for eating, you better start putting some one to cooking potatoes and cut some meat while I make some bannocks."

"Why, I can't peel potatoes," says Chuck, acting mournful. "I can't stand their soulful eyes a peeking at me."

So it come to where Kip and Scootie peeled the few potatoes that was needed while Chuck cut the meat and whiled away his time more by joking than working.

Frank didn't ride in for the noon meal. Fact is, as Uncle Bill said, he didn't expect him back till about dark on account of his visiting some friends and to see how they'd made out during the storm and flood.

The meal over with and everything scraped clean around camp, the kids put on their boots and shirts again. Kip, feeling he'd look like something that broke out of a crazy house if he went without a hat, tied a black bandana over his head, and even tho he figured he now looked like a gypsy, that would do until he got another hat to take the place of the one he lost. Then that afternoon they went and caught their horses, tinkered with 'em and their saddles for a long while, and as Uncle Bill remarked that he would like to take a little snooze they told him they'd ride to where Chuck was herding the bulls and keep him company for a spell.

To make it a longer and more interesting ride they thought of going in a roundabout way. Kip grinned and said that maybe they'd find a gold mine.

And that come closer to fact than they could know. The kids crossed a few rough ridges, and topping one high one they come to look down into a country more rough and desolate looking than any they'd ever seen. It was a sort of big basin about ten miles acrost, they figured, and looking down into it they felt as tho they was looking into a land of the dead. The breeze seemed to whisper it and like a warning for them to stay away and not disturb its quiet. Scootie sort of shivered and would of liked to've went on to where Chuck was, but Kip spotted what looked like a small dugout of cedar and rock halfways down the ridge and that stirred Scootie's curiosity, for the dugout looked deserted and might prove to be an interesting place to explore.

A band of antelope, looking more like ghosts against formations and country of their own color, stood stock still at less than five hundred yards away and watched the kids ride by. Lizards scampered here and there and one lively rattlesnake crawled into a hole before Kip could get off his horse and head it with rocks.

As was guessed, the dugout was deserted. It didn't look as tho it ever had a door, just an opening which had most likely been covered with canvas during storms.

The kids got off their horses, tied 'em well, and Kip took the lead from the bright sunlight into the dark opening. It was a little before they could see inside, and then there wasn't much to see, at first. There was a smoked corner where the fire had been built, the opening or door being the only way for the smoke to get out. Holes had been hewed out of the sandstone for shelves, and looking up at the roof it didn't seem very safe to be under, for the timbers was close to breaking under the weight of the dirt on top. There'd been cedar boughs and bunk frame below and in one corner, but with the many bones that near covered the floor it was hard to make out. The bones were from near every kind of animal that roamed that country, from pack rats to deer, and looked like the animals had either come there for shelter or been drug in by little and big cats, lynxes to lions, to feast up on or feed their young there.

By all appearances the dugout hadn't been habited by human beings for some years. Getting used to the dark, the kids then noticed a darker hole yawning at the back and into the hillside. Kip went closer, lit a match and seen it was a tunnel, a few rusted prospector's tools was still there, and with only the light of a match there was no telling how deep the tunnel was. That tunnel accounted for the ore dump they'd noticed in the front of the dugout, and whoever dug the tunnel lived at the entrance, in the dugout. The ore had been wheeled or packed thru it to be dumped down the hill in front.

Must of been valuable ore, thought the kids, for the prospector to live at the entrance of his tunnel the way he had. That tunnel would need exploring, they figured, it would be fun.

But there would have to be light, and the only way to get it was to build a fire inside or at the mouth of the tunnel. That would take away the damp dead smell that was there. They came outside, gathered some sage brush and dry cedar limbs and then going inside again with each a good armful they set up part of it to burning a little ways inside the tunnel.

The light was good but it didn't reach to the end of the tunnel, only far enough to disturb what seemed to be hundreds of bats which begin flying around close by the kids' ears and liked to scared 'em out of their wits at first. But Scootie clamping her hat down tight they squatted close to the floor of the tunnel, their hearts beating fit to bust,—but they wasn't going to quit now and let little bats scare 'em out. They remembered Uncle Bill telling 'em how it wasn't true that they got their claws into people's hair and the hair had to be cut off to get 'em loose, also it wasn't true that they're blind, for as Uncle Bill said they could see very well, night or day. They wished he was with 'em now, for they wouldn't feel so spooky in exploring the tunnel.

The bats seemed to settle down from their first confusion of the light, and the kids got up enough nerve to go a little farther in the tunnel, as far as the light of their fire would reach and there they would start another fire to light 'em on still farther. But Kip just struck a match to the dry brush he'd carried and no more than got it into a blaze when he dropped his match and blazing brush. There'd come a low and dangerous sounding growl, and looking into the dark depth of the tunnel he seen a pair of bright yellow eyes shining from the reflection of the fire.

Scootie of course heard the threatening growl and seen the eyes at the very same time Kip did, but she was quicker than Kip in deciding to get away from there and back to the entrance. There was no crawling nor minding of the bats as the two went now, they was up and going fast as they could, Scootie an arm's length in the lead.

In their fright and with the speed they was going their steps was much heavier than when they'd been crawling, they was plum careless, and that's how come that when Scootie made one step while halfways to the entrance there was a sound of giving away timber and she went down sudden and out of sight. Kip being a few feet back of her barely managed to keep his balance and from falling in right after her, but that was for only a second. There was a roar and a snarl which sounded, echoed and resounded many times louder than it was, and that took away what little balance Kip had left. Down he went and the way Scootie had.

As good luck would have it the fall wasn't deep and then again he didn't land on Scootie who'd just left a scream. It was a mighty scary happening, this screeching wild animal, whatever it was, and then this sudden dropping into space in the darkness.

Both the kids sat where they fell, close to one another and stiff with fear. Finally, not hearing any more of the wild animal's growls, Kip slowly reached in his pocket for a match and lit it, lit it just in time to look up and see a long tannish form leaping acrost the opening of the shaft him and Scootie had fell into. The match went out as quick as it had flared up.

More shaky silence for a spell and then Kip spoke in a scared whisper, "Gee, Scootie, did you see what I did?"

Scootie whispered back that she had, and she didn't have to add on that she was scared.

"It's a mountain lion," Kip whispered on, "and I'll bet he's ten feet long."

Hearing Kip's whispering sort of nerved Scootie to speak up a little and ask, "What shall we do?"

"Why, get out of here of course, if we can."

"But, but what about the lion?" says Scootie. "I'm so afraid. . . . Don't you think we'd better wait until Uncle Bill or Chuck come to look for us? We're safe from the lion here, I think."

A long tannish form leaping across the opening of the shaft

The flickering light of the small fires went dim and then dark come against the tunnel's ceiling, and Kip and Scootie went on pondering about their chances of getting away without meeting up with the lion. They knew the lion had leaped for the outside, but he might of come back and still be in the tunnel. Or there might be more lions, maybe a female with a litter of young ones.

Such would be mighty dangerous to meet up with in a den or any narrow place, Uncle Bill had said. He's said too that a lion would always try to get away if possible and never attacked a human unless cornered, or the human came up to one in too close a quarters. The tunnel would be mighty close quarters to have to pass one in, the kids thought.

With the still darkness the kids got restless and nervous. It was easy for them to imagine a lion glaring down at 'em and ready to pounce any moment. Then, to sort of break the spell, Kip lit another match to see about the depth and size of the shaft and for possible chances of getting out, also to make sure that no snarling lion's head was looking down at 'em.

It looked about ten feet to the top of the shaft, and if Kip or Scootie could manage to climb up on the other's shoulders and stand, that first one could maybe get a holt so as to get out, then the other could be helped up by the first one letting down a line of knotted clothing, belt and such.

But the thought of lion or lions made 'em ponder on some more, and as they got to thinking of waiting where they was till they was rescued it would be quite a long wait, and sort of being like in a lion's den would be mighty scary waiting. They wouldn't be missed, they figured, until Chuck came in to corral the bulls for the night, it would be about dark by then and it would be impossible for their trail to be found or followed. They would have to stay in the shaft the rest of the day, the whole long night and part of the next day before they could expect anyone to come to their rescue.

A long and dreadful wait, but the fear of the lion halfways decided 'em to do just that. At least they wasn't in no hurry in trying to get out, that is, not until Kip lit another match to see what his hand had come in contact with while squirming around.

It felt like loose joints of a bracelet or necklace in the hard rock. The light of the match showed it was loose joints, sure enough, but not of a bracelet. It was the bones of a human hand.

A shiver went up his spine and at the same time, Scootie let out a scream, for one of her hands had been resting on what she thought was a round rock, which really was a human skull.

Well, with all the other bones that went to make up the long gone human, all white and showing up spooky in the light, that was enough to near make the kids fly up out of the shaft. Awful thoughts came to 'em as they stood up against a corner of the shaft and Kip lit match after match to see what all was before 'em. They thought maybe that lions had got the poor unfortunate whose bones they was staring at, or maybe snakes, and the same fate would be theirs if they stayed.

Right then they decided quick they wouldn't be staying, but being excited as they was they couldn't get nowheres in figuring ways of getting out. They was kind of wild, like two mice swimming around in a half filled bucket of water.

Finally cooling down some, Kip lighting another match figured it out with Scootie that if he stood against the wall and she climbed on his shoulders she could reach one of the timbers that still held above the opening, and boosting her up all he could and giving her a footing with his hands she could get up over the edge.

That was the only way. But Scootie thought of the lion again, and being the first one to go up sure didn't appeal to her. In her excitement she didn't stop to think of what a predicament she'd be in if Kip went up first and she was left alone in the shaft,—her bones would in time been along with those of the prospector.

Noticing her hesitating to go up, Kip was quick to say that he would. Scootie was kind of shaky, but bracing herself up against the wall, Kip made it to scramble up on her shoulders, then also steadying himself against the wall he felt for a timber that would hold his weight, for the rest of the way up. A small slide of gravel and sand came down as he felt for one, and telling Scootie to keep her face down and keep a standing he groped on in the dark till he found a timber he figured would hold. His high heeled boots dug into Scootie's shoulders but she stood up under that, and when she felt a relief of Kip's weight and was told to put her hands under his feet and hold 'em up against the wall for a toe holt she was glad to do that, hardly minding the extra dirt that kept a sliding, and now she'd near forgot about the lion.

Finally, with Kip's hard scrambling and Scootie's steady boosting him, with new toe holts he got his shoulders and then his belly over the edge of the shaft, then he was up on top.

There was no lingering from there on. Stripping off his shirt and wide belt he tied the two together and telling Scootie to add her shirt onto that it made a rope that held and gave Kip a chance to get back from the shaft opening some, to where he could brace himself, hold on and pull.

It was no easy climbing for Scootie, but being desperate as she was to get out of the shaft, specially now that Kip was out she had more than ordinary strength, and soon enough her head was above the opening. More scrambling and then she was alongside of Kip.

Neither paused for a breath, for soon as Scootie got on her feet a low echoing growl from the dark end of the tunnel put her and Kip on a tight run for the other end and sunlight. They now was sure there was two lions and they didn't dare think of meeting the one they'd seen leaping over the shaft, they just went for all they was worth for the light and opening of the tunnel.

The way the kids run it would be doubtful if a lion would of tried to catch up with 'em. Anyhow there was none behind 'em as they come out of the tunnel and none before 'em as they sort of dived into the dugout and out thru the opening, into the sunlight. Then they didn't slow up or look either side till they got to their horses, which now looked like sent from heaven and meant safety.

With that secure feeling as Scootie begin to untie her horse, it seemed that a nice little fainting spell would kind of go well for some sort of let down right then, but Kip noticed her weaving, caught hold of her and shook her.

"Come out of it, Scootie," he says, a little rough. "Let's ride away from here first before you do any fainting, and wait till you get your shirt back on."

And that worked.

CHAPTER SEVEN

FEELING VERY SATISFIED that they'd had enough exploring for a while, Kip and Scootie took one long look at the "Land of the Dead" basin as they topped a high ridge overlooking it and then headed their horses back for camp. They came to a small spring on the way, drank, watered their horses. Then faces washed, they dusted the dirt off their clothes with their hats, and when they rode into camp late that afternoon, neither looked much the worst for their experience, only some wiser.

It was good to see old Uncle Bill there by camp as they rode in, all contented like and puttering around the fire. The sight of him gave them a sense of security and they figured that whenever they done any more exploring it would be with him if possible, for it seemed like they always got into more adventure than they wanted, hard to get out of, and which they wouldn't get into if the old cowboy was with 'em. If they did get into some adventure with him it didn't seem scary, only all the more interesting.

There was a grinning nod from him as the kids came into camp after unsaddling and hobbling their horses on good grass.

"Thought you two was on dayherd with Chuck this afternoon," he says. "Wasn't he good company?"

"We didn't go see Chuck," says Scootie. She smiled: "We went exploring."

Kip and Scootie took one long look at the "Land of the Dead" basin.

Then she went on to tell of their adventure at the dugout in the Basin, the tunnel, their fall into the shaft, the lions and the skeleton. Kip chipped in a word once in awhile, and when they got thru, Uncle Bill remarked that it was quite some adventure they had, and how he'd liked to've been with 'em.

"Yeh," says Kip. "We sure wished you'd been with us too."

Kip had pulled off one boot while speaking. Something had got in there which hurt his foot and now as he got it out he was examining a little yellow pebble which he'd found. He examined it for a while and then handed it to Uncle Bill, asking what it was.

The old cowboy took it and at a glance he seen that it was gold, a gold nugget. Kip was quite surprised and excited at that, so was Scootie, but both more surprised that Uncle Bill wasn't at all excited and looked at the nugget in the same way as if it was a plain rock pebble. He hadn't showed much interest either when told about the skeleton in the bottom of the shaft and the place where it was most likely the nugget had worked into Kip's boot top while squirming around in there.

The kids was some disappointed that Uncle Bill didn't rear up at their story and want to investigate. If not to find out about the skeleton the gold alone ought to be of plenty of interest. He was reminded pretty strong as to that, and now the kids would of liked to gone back to the tunnel and finish up the exploring, if Uncle Bill went with 'em.

But Uncle Bill wasn't much for treasure hunting, or digging up skeletons' pasts. He would of liked to've been with 'em that day but he didn't care much to make any special trip there. He was no prospector, and like most cowboys, he'd ride all his life, sometimes right by or over mineral veins that might be worth millions of dollars or a lifetime's wages, and never notice or get off his horse to hunt for it. He'd hardly know mineral if he seen it and if he did that would only mean hard digging with pick and shovel to him and the hanging up of his saddle. That's why the lack of interest.—Another thing was that no prospector was any better off than any cowpuncher, and if the prospector struck it rich in minerals the cowpuncher can also strike it the same in cattle.

With the kids' story, Uncle Bill had it summed up as to the abandoned prospect. The skeleton in the shaft was most likely that of the prospector who'd dug it, and the covering of the opening went to prove pretty well that he'd been killed for what gold he'd got and then throwed in there. If he'd died by accident it wouldn't be likely that he'd been left there when found. The shaft opening was easy to cover up, along with traces of the crime, and being the timbers was so rotted so as not to hold the kids' weight went to show that the crime had been committed too many years past for the facts to be dug up.

"And as for gold," Uncle Bill went on to say, "if any more of it was there the one or ones who covered up the shaft would of been sure to've got it. It would only be pocket gold anyway and the finding of it would be just pure luck. There's no gold veins in this part of the country that I know of nor any worth while deposits. If there was somebody would sure have known about it.

"For my part, I wouldn't raise no sweat about it nor disturb the skeleton that's been resting there so long. Of course, with some young feller like Chuck, if you mention gold to him his

Cattle used to go in there to water.

ears might perk up some and maybe get to investigating it during some winter months when there's not so much riding. But I'll bet if he got the lions he'd make more money out of their hides and bounty on 'em than all the gold he'd ever find there."

Now the kids turned their hopes to Chuck, and that cowboy hardly got the bulls corralled and himself into camp that evening when they pounced onto him about their prospect find. Kip showed him the nugget and Scootie told him about the lions, and to the kids' pleasure there was a sign of interest come to Chuck's face as he was told about it all and their experience, specially about the shaft.

"I know the tunnel you're speaking of," says Chuck, examining the nugget. "There's water at the far end and there's where the lions are watering, I guess, and getting their meat too. Cattle used to go in there to water and being the tunnel was too narrow for them to turn around and get back and they was too dumb to back out they just died there. For that reason the tunnel entrance was closed so cattle couldn't get in. That was quite some years ago, and I don't think there's any cattle in that country now.

"I used to get cattle out of there, and kill me a coyote or lynx once in a while, but I didn't come acrost no lions. If there's lions watering in the tunnel now there sure must be quite a bunch of 'em because there's nobody nor nothing to bother 'em, and being the water in the tunnel is the only water for miles around they must be making their range near and around there and keeping fat on what animals come in to drink, and get more game and cattle and horses on the outside of the basin when they get real hungry.

"It's a wonder some old cranky shemale with young ones didn't get one of you kids for her litter to play with. It's a good thing you didn't stay there tonight because they're more apt to attack then than in daytime. But if them catamounts are still there when the first chance comes that I can get away I'm sure going to get 'em. They'd ought to be worth a few months' wages in bounty."

"That's what I was telling the kids," says Uncle Bill, "They'd be worth more than what gold might be found there, if any, and I'm thinking Frank could spare you for a few days, after we get the bulls to the ranch. It'd be worth a considerable to the stockmen around to be rid of them devils, and its a wonder somebody didn't get 'em before."

"It sure is," agrees Chuck. "But then, nobody has any cause to ride in that country to know, like for instance I didn't know anything about the shaft nor of anybody dying in it, did you?"

"No," says Uncle Bill. "I only did hear of some prospector disappearing in The Basin some years ago, and that's all I know. It might not even be the same one. Nobody tries to keep track of a prospector much because he's always a rambling, and this here is a big country."

"Well, that might be worth looking into," says Chuck. "Can't tell but what that prospector might of fell in, broke a leg and couldn't get out. There might be gold all around him in that shaft."

"If that was the case, how would you account for the shaft being covered over?" asks Uncle Bill. "Wouldn't anybody look into it first and get the gold if there was any?"

"Well, the tunnel covering could of been done long after the prospector was dead and without knowledge of his being there. Maybe whoever covered it done it just so to get to the water inside the tunnel and didn't investigate the shaft."

"Nope," says Uncle Bill, "that ain't at all likely, and if I was you I wouldn't expect to get over a carload of gold out of there. Not more than two."

"Well, a gunnysackful would do," grins Chuck. "But if I dug around some I might find a little pocketful, sure enough."

Supper was being fixed as such talk was going on, and with their appetites all set to do the meal justice, along with the promising talk of more exploring of the tunnel, the kids was in high spirits and it was hard for 'em to keep still.

Then the talk switched some to Frank and when he'd be showing up, and, as with the old saying that "If you speak of a wolf you'll see his tail," there was heard the sound of hoofs and a rider showed up in the near darkness. It was Frank.

The coming of Frank put the subject of the tunnel exploring and lion hunting to rest for a while. It was replaced by the talk of the flood and the damage it had done. According to Frank it had done plenty of damage where the creek was fed by other streams coming in on both sides to swell it more, meadows was under water and covered with many inches of washed-in dirt. Some ranch houses had to be abandoned in a hurry and some smaller ones closest to the creek was washed away.

"Yep. It's done a lot of damage," Frank said, "and even Old Jones who can remember back close to seventy years can't think of any time when the creek got out of its banks and there was such a flood, and he couldn't remember of any old timers before him ever telling him of anything like it either. Jones's ranch is pretty well under water and there was near a foot of it in the main ranch house when I got there. The whole outfit had got busy and piled and carried things up to high places, and quite a lot about the ranch was ruined, but what hit Jones the most and near made the tough old booger cry was that an old top cowhorse of his which he'd pensioned and hadn't rode for some years was found tangled up in some barb wire and drowned. That near broke his heart."

Frank had visited a couple of other ranches and found things about the same all along as he did at Jones's.

"That high water sure enough done a lot of damage all right," he says, "but it also done a lot of good because the range has been pretty dry for some years and it will take some wet years to get it back to normal. This last rain was pretty general, and so was the cloudbursts," he added on. "And I hate to think of what damage they done from Jones's on down and where the creek gets to near river size even when normal."

The talk went on about the flood and there was no slowing down on it much until Uncle Bill dug up and cracked the baked clay off one of the sage chickens, then with the tasty sight and smell there was now only remarks of what damage there would be done to the chickens before the meal would be over. Parts of the clay shell went with parts of the chickens and used as plates or platters and stuck well to only the feathers and skin, leaving the meat whole and in well cooked, juicy pieces.

With a rounded piece of clayful of the chicken in one hand and a hunk of pan bread in the other, the kids forgot about their prospect find and lions for the time, and hardly listened to the talk of the flood which now came by jerks from interruptions by every mouthful.

The evening being cool the fire was kept to a cheerful blaze till the meal was over and everything put to good camp order. Then the three men squatted for a smoke and more talk, while the kids waited for an opening to bring up what was most in their minds. They wasn't much interested to hear about floods, range and stock right then.

Chuck sort of came to their rescue there, and as the talk slowed down some he ups and begins to tell of the kids' adventure and find of that afternoon. With his way of telling the story he soon got Frank's attention, with an interest to it which more than pleased the kids.

There was about the same discussions as there'd been with Uncle Bill on the subject, only Frank seemed more interested, interested about the lions because, with him, the killing of the lions meant a big saving in livestock, and whether the lions was on his range or not he would do what he could for quick riddance of 'em. Every stockman was always ready for war against lions and wolves, and to help one another to their exterminating.

Frank, like Uncle Bill, didn't put much thought to the finding of gold or what story might be around the skeleton. That was away in the past, forgotten and back to dust, and one of the many instances or tragedies that goes on everywhere, as well in cities of thousands on one square mile as with one man on a thousand square miles, like in the desert and gold countries.

As Frank also said, the getting of the lions would be a heap more valuable than whatever gold could be found within a hundred miles of the skeleton.

"All right, then," says Chuck, acting very business like. "I understand now that being you're so all fired sure 'there's no gold in them thar hills,' as the feller says, none of you will be expecting or wanting any share of what gold I may find, none but my pardners here." He pointed to Kip and Scootie.

Both Frank and Uncle Bill grinned and remarked that they'd be welcome to it, adding on that when they struck it rich and went on a spending spree or a tour around the world they wouldn't be forgetting their old friends back on the Five Barb range.

Scootie laughed and, speaking for Kip, she says: "But we don't want any share in the gold either. All we want is to finish exploring the cave, with Chuck or Uncle Bill, and see them get the lions. It would sure be fun to look for gold too, and if any is found, why Chuck can have our share, can't he, Kip?"

"Sure," Kip says, before thinking. Then, hesitating, he went on, "W-eel-l,—the only thing is I *would* like to buy a ranch some day, and—"

"Fine," grins Chuck, "now I've got a pardner to split my fortune with. We'll go fifty-fifty and pardners on the ranch too, how's that?"

It was all right with Kip, and him and Chuck shook hands to cinch the deal.

Then Scootie spoke up, "How would I do for a secretary and bookkeeper?" she asked, smiling. "You will need one to keep track of all your affairs."

Chuck looked at her and then squinted at Kip. "How about it, pardner?"

"I guess so," was all Kip said. He didn't feel any too easy at the way everybody acted, like it was all a good joke and all wanting to laugh. But it was no joke to him. He'd got the first nugget and he meant to get more.

"Now that the pardnership is decided on and a bookkeeper is appointed," says Frank, "what are you going to name the company?"

"Why, that's easy," says Chuck. "How would The Catamount Mining Company do?" he asks Kip. "Great," says Scootie, who again answered for him.

"Well, all right," says Frank, after seeing that all was agreed on, "and now I want to inform The Catamount Mining Company that they will be free to outfit at my ranch and proceed with the development of their enterprise ten days after the herd of bulls we have on hand are delivered at the ranch and scattered to their ranges.

"To make sure of the company's safety and success," he went on, "I'm appointing Mister Uncle Bill here as overseer of the younger shareholders, also to act in the capacity of chief cook and bottle washer.

"Now, before the meeting is over, those not in favor speak up or forever keep peace."

Not a chirp was heard from any of the solemn-acting four, and then using a rock for a gavel, Frank pronounced the meeting over.

"Everybody to their soogans," he ordered, "for tomorrow morning we shove the herd acrost the stream."

CHAPTER EIGHT

I T TOOK SOME LITTLE TIME for the kids to get to sleep that night.
The crossing of the cattle and the going on would be very
much to their liking, for with kids, like with most older people,
forever going is always interesting. There was whisperings of what
fun the days ahead would hold, the getting back and seeing the
ranch again. Then their own ranch, as they called it, and which
they'd started to build up from the first log building which had
been on that land and built by their grandfather. In a few days
they could also look forward to the trip back to the tunnel for
more exploring and the getting of the lions.

It all looked as plenty of interesting doings for some time to
come, starting in the morning, and they finally went to sleep
thinking on that.

It seemed that they'd hardly closed their eyes when Uncle
Bill rattled a tune on the only tin lid in camp and woke up the
minor officers of The Catamount Mining Company. The sun was
up and warm when they blinked out of their tepee, it would be
hot before it got very high, and it would be well to get the fat
bulls on the trail before then.

The creek had gone down a considerable the day before, and
during the night and was near normal. It would go down some

Uncle Bill rattled a tune on the only tin lid in camp.

more by the time breakfast would be over, camp broke up and the bulls drove to the crossing.

"Well, how's the Catamounts this morning?" says Frank to the kids as the two came down from the spring where they'd washed.

"Hard as hard rock," grins Kip, and "fit as a fiddle," says Scootie, following up.

"Well, that's good, and better not fill up with too many of Bill's pancakes. The creek is pretty deep and swift yet and in case there's swimming to be done they might weigh you down. But being it would be up to your horses to do the swimming and they won't be getting any of the pancakes, it might not make much difference.

Uncle Bill, overhearing the advising remarks, was quick with a comeback, that any little sin was a heap heavier than any of his pancakes, and such being the case, Frank had better have a powerful good swimming horse under him before starting to cross the stream.

"And you'd need a barge, you old sinner," grins Frank as he took a good mouthful of pancake and bacon.

The morning meal over with, and the leavings left to the chipmunks, if the magpies didn't get there first, it didn't take long to break up camp and have it ready to pack. With enough cooked grub tied at the back of the saddles to do for the day, Chuck was to pack up what all had been borrowed on the pack horse and return it to the Morrison ranch. Frank, Uncle Bill, and the two kids would drive on with the bulls and Chuck could catch up with 'em that day. But before leaving he would help with the crossing of the bulls.

The bulls had been left out of the corral and to graze at the break of day, and now they was ready to ramble. It was no trouble getting them to the creek, but to put 'em acrost it right is where the ticklish part would come, for, on account of the water being so swift, the leaders would have to be headed well up the stream and the others to follow so that with bucking the swift current none would be swept past and below the crossing on the other side. If that crossing was missed, and with the banks being steep and brushy on both sides many would be apt to drown in the deep and tangled places as they'd be swept down the creek and before they could come to another place to get out.

It would take another couple of days before the creek would be down to normal and safer, but the thought of waiting didn't please none much, and Frank figured it was now safe enough to tackle.

What little fear he had was for the kids, and while advising 'em as to what to do he was careful not to let 'em think there was any danger, less than in taking a bath, and for them not to be afraid of the water, even if it might come up to their waist and their horses have to swim.

"It's nice warm weather anyway," he laughed, "and along about noon I'm thinking you'll be wishing there was another creek to cross so you could cool off some."

At the crossing he loosened their cinches a little, then advised 'em to stay behind the bulls and follow 'em acrost, not to mind if any of 'em broke back or went downstream, him and Uncle Bill and Chuck would take care of that. He pointed out a way for the kids to cross; and if the bulls got to be hard to handle while in the middle of the stream they was to go right on, make a half circle up the stream and then come down with it to the opening on the other side.

"Don't look down at the water," says Frank. "That would only make you dizzy. Look up and head your horse to where you want to go, and be sure not to jerk or try to turn your horse too quick where it's deep or he might turn over in the swift water. The same if you get rattled, don't go to pulling up on the reins. If you want to grab on to anything grab on to his mane, the sadle horn, or anything but pulling tight on the reins. The horse will get you out if you ride far enough upstream and then give him his head."

The kids was a little nervous after listening to all the "don'ts" from their Uncle Frank, but that had to be, and looking at the swift running stream didn't help calm 'em down any.

"Nothing to it," says Frank, as he rode to start the bulls. "Just do as I said and all will be fine."

The starting of the bulls to cross was easier to think of than to do, for, after considerable milling into the edge of the stream there was none could be made to take to the deeper water and specially up the stream, as was wanted.

Frank, fearing that the bulls would cause some trouble while crossing, and now himself some nervous for the kids, decided it would be best not to take them and the bulls across at the same time. The bulls alone would be a plenty to handle in case anything went wrong.

Uncle Bill felt the same way about it, and so, Frank told him to haze the kids acrost first, and if possible, him and Chuck would get the cattle to follow their lead.

The kids was for staying back and helping all they could, and to ease their feelings, Uncle Bill told 'em they would be helping, by taking the lead. While the cattle was milling, Uncle Bill told the kids to follow him and not get below stream from him. Then the three circled close by the milling cattle and into the stream they went, the while Frank and Chuck tried to work out some leaders to follow. Uncle Bill and the kids was up and midstream when some leaders finally did line out after 'em and the others started to follow.

Uncle Bill, looking back and grinning encouragement at the kids, grinned some more at the sight of the bulls following, and remarked to that effect. But his words didn't register with 'em right then, for as he spoke, their horses struck swimming waters which of a sudden got up well above their waists and took the breath out of 'em. With the loss of footing the horses started going down stream but swimming strong against the stream and steady bearing for the other side they soon struck bottom and footing again, along with the kids getting their breath.

Getting safely across was easy from there and making sure of that, Uncle Bill told the kids to go on ahead, then waving back to the cattle as to help there he started to turn his horse, just as his horse struck a hole and was in swimming waters again. Consequences was that the horse, without footing, was turned over by the swift current, just as Frank had warned the kids of.

The kids didn't get to see much of that, only the splashing of upturned hoofs, and when they got safely across and looked back, Uncle Bill was alongside his horse which now was right side up again, but the both had missed the crossing and was being carried down stream.

Consequences was that the horse, without footing,
was turned over by the swift current.

It was an exciting time for a spell, for two of the bulls had broke loose and was also going down the stream of the now deep creek, not far behind Uncle Bill. Frank and Chuck seeing they could do nothing about the two bulls or Uncle Bill for the time stayed with the bulls they had and without much more trouble got 'em across to where Kip and Scootie, round eyed and pale, was on high ground and sitting on their horses.

Chuck no more than rode up out of the creek when he put his horse on a high lope on along the bank to catch up with

Uncle Bill and head off the two bulls, if there come a chance. Frank, riding up to the kids, told 'em to watch the bulls and not to worry about Uncle Bill, that he'd been in many worse predicaments before, and him and Chuck would soon get a rope to him and get him out. Then he rode down to join Chuck.

But getting a rope to the old cowboy was no easy thing to do, for the brush being so thick along the creek bank it was impossible to ride thru in some places, and more impossible to throw a rope. Then the creek banks being so steep there was no trail openings to water, only narrow deer slides and them was easy to get in, but not to get out. It would of been useless and only foolish for either Frank or Chuck to take one of the deer slides into the creek, for either one would of been in the same predicament Uncle Bill now was, and could be of no help to him there.

The only and best thing that could be done was to ride along the bank, watch for an opening and get there ahead of Uncle Bill so as to throw him a rope in case he couldn't turn his horse to get out.

The two rode along, catching a glimpse of him every once in a while and hollering words of encouragement. Uncle Bill would hear and sometimes answer back, but not at all in the way of a drowning man. Fact is, he was near enjoying it, just floating along with the current and a good mane holt on his horse, which was cool headed enough to swim only just so as to keep floating.

The two bulls coming along behind seemed to be swimming at the same ease, and once in a while looking back at 'em, Uncle Bill figured it was lucky he was ahead of 'em because at the first opening where they might be able to get out he could maybe turn 'em that direction.

The swimmers had gone down the creek about half a mile when it begin to widen, and looking ahead, Uncle Bill thought he was coming to a lake, but reasoning some he come to figure it was only a beaver dam. But it was near a quarter of a mile wide. The current was slowing down some and was splitting to go on both sides of the back waters from the dam. Now, Uncle Bill thought, was the time to see that the bulls took to the right side of the creek and went with the current, for then they'd soon be out of the creek bed and get footing with the overflowing waters on the bank.

It would be tough and dangerous work to try and head off the bulls if they took the left split of the current, then they would be back on the same side they was started from. So, hoping for the best and that they would follow his lead, Uncle Bill reined his horse to swim along with the right current and close to the bank. If the bulls followed him only a short ways he'd have 'em, because then they wouldn't want to swim acrost the deep still water backed by the dam to get to the far side. If they took to the left current that's just what he'd have to do to head 'em off and turn 'em to the right.

But there didn't seem to be no need of any fear as to that, for the bulls followed on the old cowboy's lead as if their life depended on it, which it did, some. Then the current overflowing from the backwaters of the dam begin to turn into the brush, out of the creek bed and onto its banks, and of a sudden Uncle Bill's horse got to touching the bank, got his footing and stood stirrup high above the rushing waters.

It was a great feeling for both man and horse to touch good earth again, even tho it was mighty soft and boggy. In the thick entanglement of brush, trees, and washed in limbs and tree trunks piled high along the bank, Uncle Bill had to do considerable manoeuvring to make any headway in getting out. He couldn't of gone any place by getting on his horse, for as it was and afoot he had to stoop most of the time to get anywheres, then often only to bump up against places where the brush was so thick he'd have to turn back the way he come and try another way. Leading his horse he sometimes couldn't get him thru on account of some heavy limbs which couldn't be got around or bent up and would catch the saddle.

As he wormed his way thru the jungle of thick brush, most of the time hip deep in the rushing waters he'd sometimes come to a hole where it was neck deep, but being that limbs was always very handy he didn't have to worry about gulping too much water at one time. His horse stayed mighty close to him at such deep places, sometimes too close in his hurry to get thru, and Uncle Bill would then have to get alongside his neck again to keep from being tromped on.

As for the bulls there was no wondering of their location, for with their scrambling, wallowing, and crashing their way thru the brush they made a noise that was easy heard, and never very far from where Uncle Bill was fighting his own way thru. He had no fear of losing them now. They would never try to get back on the other side, he knew, and they would soon work their way out of the brush to where they could see around and up on his open ground, better and quicker than if a rider tried to get 'em out, and no rider could of gone thru places they did, even if afoot and leading his horse.

Once in a while, Uncle Bill heard the hollers of Frank and Chuck and he hollered back at 'em in the plainest way he could that he was all right and coming out. They heard and pretty well understood what he said, and when they come to where the waters spread out, covering the brushy flat on the side of the beaver dam, and hearing the old cowboy's hollers in that entanglement they knew that he'd got footing in the thick of it and would soon come out. They also knew they could be of no help to him there, and so long as they heard his holler now and again and getting closer they was satisfied to just sit on their horses and watch down the brushy, water-covered bottom from their higher ground.

Then they begin to hear of crashing thru the brush, and knowing that wasn't all of Uncle Bill's doings, they got to thinking about the bulls, that it must be them.

"Guess the old boy is bringing them out, too," grins Chuck.

"I'm thinking they're bringing themselves out," says Frank, "and I'll bet we'll see them quite a bit before we do Bill."

Frank was right, and soon enough there was splashing in muddy waters, more crashing of brush, and the two husky wild eyed bulls came out and up to higher land, like two scared animals that just escaped a swampy death trap, which was right.

The two cowboys sat still on their horses, for riding towards 'em right then and trying to turn 'em in with the other bulls while they was all spooked up would only make 'em worse, hard to handle, and get 'em on the fight. It would be best to let 'em cool off, even if they'd just got out of plenty of cool water.

The two bulls got up on high ground, their slick hides shining and still dripping wet, and at seeing the riders they threw up their heads, shook their horns and blowed at 'em and then trotted off. But it wasn't for long, they was too full of water, and seeing that the riders wasn't following they got down to a walk and doing some more looking around. Then up country, near a mile away, they seen the bunch they'd been with, and slowly started that direction.

The two bulls got up on high ground.

The riders' attention was drawed back by more crashing of brush and splashing of water, a loud holler and after awhile Uncle Bill was seen winding his way to the edge of the bottom, then also on up for high ground. Frank and Chuck rode to meet him as he came out, and there wasn't much more than an exchange of grins as the three met.

Seeing that the bull herd was grazing quiet and the two bunch quitters was going to join it again, the three didn't see no hurry to getting back to help the kids, and so they went to taking off their clothes and wringing the water out of 'em as much as they could, even to their socks. With that and some fanning to the warm breeze, along with the help of the sun, the clothes soon got fairly dry, dry enough to put on again, and as they would be riding along, shaps a hanging free to also dry in the breeze, it wouldn't be long when there'd be no feeling of moisture in 'em, only dried mud on the saddles and shaps to show of the deep waters and mud of the creek crossing.

"Well," says Uncle Bill to Frank, as the three got on their horses again, "I guess you was right about me needing a barge on account of my sins weighing more than my pancakes—" he grinned—"I guess I could of used one in great style today all right."

"And I guess it was a good thing I did have a powerful swimming horse under me," Frank added on. "Like you said, I'd sure need one."

"According to that," Chuck chips in, "I'm as free of sin as Kip and Scootie. I had a poor swimming horse and Bill's pancakes to be blamed if anything went wrong. No sins is what saved me."

"Yeh, sure. You're right as sin," grins Frank.

It was a happy pair of kids that watched the three riders loping up to them. It was seen that they'd wrung out their clothes too while they was watching the cattle, and they had a better chance to dry 'em well, for they had more time.

Now that the cattle was crossed, all together again, ready to move on, and there was no more trouble to be expected along the trail, Chuck could go back, get the pack horse and outfit and return it to the Morrison folks. The way he'd have to go, back to the Morrison ranch and then where camp would be made for the night, that would be a forty-mile ride for Chuck and he couldn't be expected to catch up until late that day, or at camp that night.

"We'll make it to The Gap easy enough before sundown," says Frank to Chuck, "and we'll corral and camp there tonight."

"Yes," Uncle Bill added on, "and you better not let Miss Julie keep you too long and spoil your nighty-night's sleep."

"No, father," says Chuck, like a very obeying son, "I promise I will not."

With that and a wave of his hand to the kids he rode away. The four then rode closer to the creek and watched to make sure of his crossing it again. But he had no trouble there, just another good wetting as his horse had to swim for a few yards, and then he was on the other side, waved again and rode on to where the pack horse had been tied to a tree by the camp outfit.

The four turned their horses towards the cattle and started 'em on the move along the road to The Gap, another camp on the way to the home ranch.

CHAPTER NINE

I T WAS DURING THE HEAT of the day, the sun at its highest and
beating straight down. The cattle had been left to graze and
lay during that spell, the horses grazed with dragging bridle
reins or at rope's length, while the riders made up a light meal
out of what had been packed at the back of their saddles. Over
half of the distance to The Gap and where camp was to be
made for the night, was covered. There'd been no water on the
high plain for grazing and resting, and they would soon be put
on the move again.

Frank was about to stir to get to his horse and adjust his saddle to start on the move, when looking the direction of The Gap he seen a dust, and then an automobile coming down the road.

"By golly," he says, standing up, "here comes the car with grub, camp outfit and all. We're in luck, even if it is some late to do us much good."

The car came right along and soon to a stop within a short distance of the riders, and a smiling cowboy hopped out.

"Sorry I couldn't make it any sooner, Frank," he begins, "but you know why. . . . Got stuck twice yesterday and had to walk back to the ranch both times for a team to get me out. When I got stuck the third time I just let 'er set, it was getting too far to walk back."

"Well," says Frank, "that ain't surprising me none, I expected that the rains would make some places mighty boggy for a car to get thru. But how did you get out after the third time you got stuck?"

"I dug out, all yesterday afternoon and part of this morning. I slept by the car last night, and"—the cowboy grinned—"I was glad there was plenty of grub with me. A feller sure needs it, wrassling a muck stick like I had to."

"Yes, and I'm glad you're here," says Frank. "Now you can go back, as far as The Gap and set up camp there. You know the spot, near the spring and above where the water runs into the corral. I expect we'll get there along about sundown."

"I'd like to swap jobs with anybody on a good horse," hinted the cowboy as he grinned and went back to the car. He had no hopes of being taken up on that.

The car was well on its way when the cattle was again put on the move and that afternoon was spent in good, long, and slow driving. The kids rode pretty well apart, sometimes one with Frank, the other with Uncle Bill or the other way around, and the conversations that went on during the drive done well to keep away any monotony, for it seems like a person enjoys talking more, and with more sense, while riding slow behind a herd than at any talking fiesta or gathering.

The country around added on to pleasure of riding and talking. Light clouds came to make shade spots over the plain, rolling hills and snow-capped timbered hills, and even tho it was hot and still and swarms of flying ants, heel and nose flies pesticated around once in awhile and could very well be got along without none seemed to be minding the pests much. There was too much of the good for a little bad to do any disturbing.

The cattle was now getting into scrubby foothill timber and up long sloping ridges towards the mountains. As the sun begin throwing long shadows and tipping a tall snowcapped peak the cattle was drove thru a thick grove of aspens and then left to graze in the tender grass above it. The set up tent by the car, and smoke of the camp fire could be seen just a little ways further on, also the cowboy busy tinkering around there.

That cowboy got his job on a good horse that evening, and without having to swap with the one of driving the car. For Frank loaned him his horse and told him, keep watch on the grazing bulls until dark and time to corral them for the night. Him and Uncle Bill would have a good supper ready by then, and as for Kip and Scootie, they wanted to help by watching the bulls themselves, but Frank reminded 'em that they was still city softies and had better call it a day and rest up some.

With fresh grub, plenty of skillets and pots to cook it in, regular tin plates, cups, and utensils to eat it out of, a good bait was mixed up and got away with that evening. Then the bulls was corralled for the night afterwards, horses picketed and all went to rest, without any sound of Chuck riding in.

The camp was asleep when he did ride in, along in the middle of the night and picketed his horse, and now he was asleep when the camp woke up at daybreak and Uncle Bill stirred the fire with more wood and to a blaze. When he got things to cooking and halfways going he let out a holler of "roll out and come and

And now he was asleep when the camp woke up at daybreak.

get it" that echoed a long ways in the still air and thru the deep canyoned mountains.

The holler was for Chuck's benefit, as Frank and the cowboy had long ago turned the bulls out of the corral to water and graze before they'd be moved on,—even Kip and Scootie was by the fire, watching and trying to help Uncle Bill with the breakfast.

Chuck rolled out of his one blanket, all dressed but for his boots. He'd kept his hat on for a night cap, as cowboys most always do, when sleeping outside, and when Uncle Bill hollered he was up and ready to ride before the echo of that holler died down.

"This is what I call style and service." He yawned and stretched. "Breakfast most ready, coffee waiting and the herd already on feed. Some day, when I get rich I'm going to have things just like this."

Then to sort of escape what sharp remarks he knew would be coming from Uncle Bill he ambled away to the cool little mountain stream and begin splashing water on his face, like to drown any noise that would be coming his direction.

All hands, with plates and cups, was soon on the job and helping themselves with *ham and eggs* that morning, and about the only talk thru the meal was from Uncle Bill and Chuck a trying to get the leverage on one another. It was about to a tie when the meal was over and all was making ready to move. Then Frank walked to where the kids was saddling their horses.

"Well youngsters," he begins, careful of what he was going to say, "I think it would be a good idea for you two to hop in the car and ride it the rest of the way on into the ranch instead of with us and the cattle. You could be there in less than two hours, where it will take us till dark. Then you could clean up, change clothes and rest good. Martha will sure be glad to see you.—As for your horses they'll have it easy just following along with the cattle."

Frank had figured before he started to speak that his idea wouldn't be so welcome with the kids, and as he seen how they took it he near wished that he hadn't mentioned it. But he'd only thought for their comfort, and as he told 'em he'd planned for them to ride only half a day from the start of the trip and take the car from there on.

But Scootie, to the relief of Kip, came to the front and would have none of the car, said that she'd seen and rode enough of them gas eaters to last her a life time, and being there was only one more day's drive she wasn't going to miss out on it.

Kip stood pat like agreeing with Scootie, and that meant loser out for Frank. He grinned, thinking all the more of 'em for their stand.

"All right," he says, "but I'm telling you *now* it's going to be a long day's drive, and you two had better think it over before the car passes us on the way to the ranch. We'll be starting with the cattle right soon, and it'll be about an hour by the time Mac picks up camp and starts back. Better think it over."

There was no thinking it over with the kids. If anything they was afraid that their Uncle Frank would insist on them taking the car. But they was on the job when the cattle was started and it was their aim to stay with them.

116

Which they did, and when the car passed 'em on the road later and no more was heard from Frank, they felt mighty relieved, and settled down to enjoy that day's ride.

That day's drive did prove to be a long one, but in prettier and cooler country than the day before. There was more trees and water, and when come time for a light noon lunch, resting and grazing of the cattle, it was in a grassy and shady little meadow this time and by a cool clear stream, the kind of a spot any outdoor man would dream of as a real camping place.

Many such places was passed as the cattle was moved on again, pretty and changing scenery which the kids more than enjoyed and of the kind they always remembered and yearned for whenever away from it, like when in the big city.

They rode on, taking all in and enjoying everything. But along towards late afternoon they begin to get tired, more and more so with every long winding mile, and about all they got to looking at as they now rode was the distance ahead and the powerful backs of the bulls slowly covering it. Before the sun went down and they come to more familiar country they got to thinking that not only the ranch but the big valley it was in was a lot farther than before, as tho it had all moved. And before dark, when they did finally get to see the valley, and the ranch still away off, they'd about as soon slid off their horses and curled up to sleep right there on the prairie sod as rode on, for slow riding behind cattle is very tiresome for anyone not used to it, much more so than faster and with change of gaits.

But the both was careful not to show they was tired, and whenever there was any conversation with either of the Uncles or Chuck they done their best to show as much a lively interest as they had that morning.

Finally, like they'd never get there, the tall pole gate of a strong fence was reached. Chuck rode ahead to open it and the bulls was drove thru into the pasture, where they would be for the night. From there they rode on at a faster gait and soon the big corrals at the ranch was reached, the horses unsaddled, and turned into another pasture, and then all five started for the ranch house.

The kids kind of livened up some then, and there was a grand and happy howdedo as them and Martha met again. Being that Mac had drove in early that forenoon and told her of the coming of the kids, along with Frank and Uncle Bill, she'd got busy, done some extra and fancy cooking and was well prepared for them all. The meal was very much enjoyed and done justice to, for it'd been a long time since the light noon lunch.

The kids stayed with it as long as the three grown men, but the effect it had on 'em wasn't for staying so long and doing much talking afterwards. Their eyelids got to feeling like there was weights on 'em, and Martha catching Kip at nodding a couple of times called it a day for them.

"Why, it must be away past their bed time," she says, and speaking to Frank, "I expect you was in the saddle before sun up, as usual, and do you realize that's before four o'clock and that you didn't get here till nine this evening? That's about seventeen hours in the saddle, and the poor children must be all wore out, not being used to it like you men are. It's after half past ten now, you all go to bed and I'll take the children to their rooms."

"All right, Miss Martha," says Frank. "But I did warn the youngsters that it would be a long ride"—he grinned—"and I think they're ready for another now, on a feather tick—Good night."

The three filed out, and it was only a short time after the kids was taken to their rooms and seen the cool beds ready there that they undressed and was soon, not in dreamland but dead to the world.

The kids had been sleeping with their clothes on for three nights, the longest such a spell in their lives. They'd slept that way when lost in the big sage brush flat the summer before, but that'd been for only one night, and it had been dry and warm there. This time it'd been just the opposite, soaked to the skin, shivering and cold for the first two nights. The third night wasn't so bad. But now, with all the chance to shed off good and roll into a clean dry bed was something very welcome and to be appreciated, more than they'd ever had anytime before.

They sure of course liked to sleep out in the open, but the sudden change from their soft city home beds, then pullman to soggy wet ground and clothes and shivering with cold was a little too much for a starter.

The kids, sometimes thinking of their folks while in that damp condition, would near have to laugh at how their mother would take on and fret if she knew of their fix. She'd got a doctor at once and would have had 'em go thru all kinds of directions and taking medicines to prevent what all she'd felt sure they'd be catching after such an experience. They'd maybe been kept in bed for a week or so.

But the kids was themselves surprised that, as Scootie put it, they didn't feel no ill effects of any kind from their exposure, and when they got out of bed late the next morning, washed and slipped on fresh dry clothes there was nothing ailing 'em that they could feel excepting an emptiness in the pit of the stomach, and Martha was well prepared with the necessary to ease that. A good long spell at the appetizing table she'd set for 'em, and with her smiling company, talk, and looking after their every need as they et soon made 'em feel as good as new and ready for more adventure, till noon time.

And Martha, watching 'em for any sign of sickness, soon seen that the only chance for them to be sick would be to make 'em that way, by holding 'em inside, smothering 'em with blankets and giving 'em medicine. She laughed to herself at the thought that that would be plain torture and would sure enough make 'em so sick as to near kill 'em.

Scootie stayed to talk and visit with her after the late breakfast and, even against Martha's wishes, went to help her with the dishes. That all being women's talk and work now, Kip hit for outside to meander around, sort of looking the familiar ranch over and enjoying all of being there again to his heart's content.

Martha had said that their Uncle Frank, Bill, Chuck, and Mac had already rode away a couple of hours before, and so, Kip didn't go to looking for 'em. He had an idea that they'd gone to take the bulls out of the pasture and scatter 'em to different herds on the range, but he wasn't sure. He didn't know which way they'd went, and figuring he'd have a hard time finding or catching up with 'em he let riding go for that forenoon. He felt he'd had plenty of that to do him for the time anyhow.

Scootie must of felt the same way, or else was wanting another woman's company for a change. Anyway she didn't show up during his meandering and he was left by his lonesome, not at all feeling that way. He stopped by the cook house to say hello to the cook there and talk to him a spell, then went on down to the stables and corrals where he was bound to wind up at.

And where, as Scootie figured, she was bound to find him, which she did a little later. She found him by a little stream which run thru a feeding corral, and busy at washing the caked mud off his saddle and shaps. There was no mud on her outfit, for her horse hadn't fell and slid on the muddy earth as Kip's had, so she busied herself at doing nothing but perching herself on the corral fence, looking around at the big spread of the buildings and ranch and the country surrounding, like wondering what next in such all promising land.

*She busied herself at doing nothing but perching
herself on the corral fence.*

CHAPTER TEN

THE KIDS, NOW BOTH RIGHT SIDE UP with care again after a good night's rest, a fresh and clean change of clothes, then a great breakfast, felt right up to snuff and very much at home again on the old Five Barb ranch. The drive to it was now only a good experience, and even tho rough and scary at times they was glad they went thru it, for such all stacks up to the good in a person's lifetime.

Scootie perched up on the corral smiled down at Kip as she noticed what horses had been left in the corral, only a heavy work team and one old saddle horse which was used for wrangling. The others kept at the ranch was out in the pasture, theirs along with 'em.

"I see they didn't expect us up very early this morning," she says to him, "and that we wouldn't care to ride for a while, because they didn't leave our horses in the corral."

"Well, they figured right, I guess," says Kip. "You wouldn't care to go right on riding this morning, would you?"

"Well, not exactly," she smiled some more. "Maybe this afternoon."

But neither rode that afternoon, not even tho they had a chance to. Uncle Bill and Frank rode in a little late that noon, the kids waited to eat the meal with 'em, and before then, while meandering around the ranch, they'd come to the old log house with the caved in roof, the first house that'd been built on the Five Barb range and by the elder Powers. Frank and their Dad, Ben, had been born in that house, but now it had been deserted for near thirty years.

The sight of the old building and what all Kip and Scootie had planned to do with it had sort of took way their interest to riding for that day, and now they'd decided to go on where they'd left off and do some more planning and work on it. They'd started that the summer before and made good headway at it, cleaned out all the dirt and fallen rotted timbers from roof and floor and leaving only the sound and heavy wall logs which was a foot thru and high and dry on a rock foundation. They was good for another life-time or two.

Kip had been the first to discover, or notice the old building while riding by it one day the summer before. It hadn't been easy to see on account of being so surrounded with tall cottonwoods and other trees, but once Kip seen it and begin to look, the idea had of a sudden come to his mind of fixing up the place and making his camp there, fixing it up something like old Zeb's camp, the old cowboy who was keeping tab on the thoroughbred herd of Five Barb cattle and where him and Scootie came on to the time they got lost and while drifting, afoot, thru the big country.

Scootie hadn't showed much interest in the old building Kip had located at first, nor of his idea of fixing it up. But as he meant it and started to work on it she also begin to take as much interest as Kip had, for she seen where one end of the old building would suit her mighty well, if fixed up, and with pictures coming to her mind as to how she could fix it, how much fun she'd have doing it, like a place of her very own and all, she'd pitched right in and went to work with Kip.

With wheelbarrow, pick and shovel and an ax they played as pioneers and first settlers on the land, and they both worked like beavers, leaving Uncle Bill setting high and dry as to his responsibility of going on long rides with 'em and watching over 'em as they rode, for they wasn't riding much any more for the time, and even tho they kept their horses near, that was just precaution, they said, in case some warring Indians come to swooping down on 'em, like they did on the early settlers.

Uncle Bill often had to smile at their make-believe, but as they'd kept at it, tugging away at the rotted timbers, sweating at pick and shovel work in clearing the inside of fallen dirt and all, he seen where a lot was meant along with the making believe, and it was practical and useful work too, like for a place of their own and of their own building.

The old cowboy would ride in on 'em and palaver with 'em once in a while, but he wasn't expected or asked to help. Only once in a while they would ask his advice as to this and that, and then one day as he'd peacefully rode in on 'em he was simply told that they'd decided to make him cow foreman of their outfit. Uncle Bill felt very much honored, as he said, but he wondered where was all their cattle.

At that he was informed and to make believe that they was "monarchs of all they surveyed." All and far as they could see, Kip had added on, and that of course took in all the cattle and horses and the land in sight, whether that all was Uncle Frank's

With wheelbarrow, pick and shovel and an ax they played
as pioneers and first settlers on the land.

or anybody else's. The cattle could be imagined they was buffalo whenever the case come when they should be, and the loose horses on the range as wild mustangs.

Uncle Bill grinned and understood. He seen where he would have a part to play too and was included in their make believe idea. That pleased him a considerable, for he'd sort of felt left out and was afraid of not having much more to do with 'em since they'd started their new venture. He'd missed their company more than he thought he would, and now being in on the play with 'em he was more than glad to accept the foremanship of the outfit and also being made chief scout when after a bunch of horse thieves. So, that way he rode in on 'em whenever he had a chance, when there wasn't too much riding for him to attend to.

Now with the going on with the ranch as their own and their play, and after they would clean up the last winter's accumulation of drifted in dirt, there come the question of getting good heavy timbers for ridge logs and for other logs that needed replacing, and instead of riding they would be busy to looking the place over again, and figure out just what they'd need in logs to fix the place up. They of course couldn't begin to get the logs themselves, not even with the help of Uncle Bill, and some more had to be figured on there, to get the help,—help again to get the heavy logs up on the roof and grooved to fit. Then later on there'd be the need of lumber for roof and floor, also doors, windows and all such that's used to finish putting a house together. Uncle Frank would have to be seen about all of that, and now that they got to thinking about all that'd be needed and the work to be done they got to wondering if their Uncle Frank would help them finish up what they'd started. Supposing he just sort of laughed at 'em and called their work just kids' play?

As they thought on the subject they figured it queer that that hadn't come to their minds before, before they done all the work they had on the place, and they finally got to see that the reason they didn't was all on account of their excitement and the fun they'd had in doing the work. They still had the same interest they first had and would now have the same if not more fun in finishing up the place, also make good use of it during summers by living there, besides having the pleasure of fixing it to their taste and as their own.

The old building had been built as two good sized cabins, with a good space between, like for a porch which was roofed over and connecting from one cabin to the other.

Kip and Scootie had no argument as to which cabin each would use, and the simple reason was that Scootie picking on hers first on account she liked it best left no choice for Kip as to the other, but as good luck would have it he also liked his best. There was a fireplace in his.

Getting along so well as a starter, each got to figuring how they would fix up their own cabin. Kip had his own ideas for his and so did Scootie for hers, and both agreed that neither would interfere with the other's plans that way but would help one another whenever help was needed.

They also agreed on a spot to build a corral and shed for their horses, for they would have to have them near during the day. There'd also have to be a pole fence around the place to keep loose stock out and big enough to pasture their horses in when they wanted to. As to the grounds right close to the house, Kip left that altogether to Scootie. If she wanted to plant flowers or anything that'd be up to her. As for the rest he was just for keeping the weeds down and letting the grass grow to pasture their horses on. They'd be the lawn mowers.

Everything was figured down pat, even to the inside finishing touches such as the kind of curtains which Scootie said she would have. Kip didn't want any curtains but he'd have other things which Scootie wouldn't want. But that was agreeable because it was each their own place and neither had any say as to the other's fixings.

But the main question which had 'em figuring and kept bobbing up as they planned was to get all the necessary help and material to go on with completing the work. It was plain to them that their Uncle Frank was the only one who could answer and decide on the question. His yes or no would have all to do about it, and getting up enough nerve to talk to him on the subject, picking out the right time and doing the right kind of talk on it would need some more figuring, and in any way it would be a ticklish job to tackle.

Kip done his best to help with the figuring on that, but he wouldn't be taking no lead on the tackling. Scootie would be the best at that, as she'd proved quite a few times already, before and without giving him a chance to say a word. Now she would be welcome to take the lead. He'd of course be with her and do all he could to help her, chipping in a word or two if necessary but he'd only come second on the subject, and to his surprise and pleasure that was agreeable with her.

But waiting for the chance to get to talk to their Uncle Frank alone and at a good time was another thing, and for that reason and while watching for the chance there was a couple of days following when there wasn't much interesting doings for the kids. The goings on at the ranch was as a good average and had always kept 'em on the jump and rearing to go, but now they didn't seem to have much heart in anything, they wasn't so anxious to be riding up the mountains and on the summer range with Uncle Bill as before, nor ride any other place or even ride at all. The old cowboy noticed that and he wondered.

He wondered some more when out on another ride one day, to sort of keep tab on the new bulls. Frank was along, and when come time for the two older riders to separate and each make their own circle thru the scattered bunches of cattle the kids both went with Frank, when they usually always went with Uncle Bill. It wouldn't of been noticed if one had rode along with Uncle Bill but the both of 'em going with Frank made the old cowboy feel sort of queer and like he'd been deserted.

Frank also wondered some at both of the kids going with him and he come near remarking to them about it, but thinking it over he got to figuring they might have some reason, which he soon enough found out they had.

"Uncle Frank," Scootie begins, right out of a clear sky. Her own voice near scared her.

"Yes," says Frank, looking at her, and now knowing for sure that something was up.

"Well, Uncle Frank," she went on, braver now that she'd started, "have you noticed any changes about the old deserted

*Both of 'em going with Frank made the old cowboy feel sort of queer
and like he'd been deserted.*

log house in the cottonwood grove lately? I mean the one above where the big spring makes a turn down to the corrals."

"No, I haven't been close to the old place," says Frank, "not lately, but I did notice last fall that you kids had been doing some kind of work there, clearing up around and such, and Bill tells me that you're at it again. What are you two planning to do there anyway," he grinned, "start a ranch?"

That gave Scootie all the lead she needed, and as they rode along she went right on to tell all that her and Kip had planned to do, how they would fix the old place all up and live there during the summers to come, if that was agreeable to him, if not some one else could maybe make use of it. She sort of went around the make believe parts and such, but Frank figured there would naturally be some play along with the work, and that would be all right.

He listened well and with a lot more interest than he showed, and the good part come when she did talk so as to *make* him interested and about all she could get out of him was an agreeing grunt once in a while, like to show he was listening, some, all the while having a hard time to keep from showing the interest he felt or laughing at her so sincere and sort of pleading talk. It was mighty good talking, thought Frank to himself.

The hardest part for Scootie was when she come to the part where her and Kip would be needing some of his help for men to do the getting and placing of the logs, then the lumber and all that would be necessary to fix up the old place and make it comfortable to live in.

Right there at that point, Frank was true enough hardly listening to Scootie. He'd caught her words of "fixing up the old place." That kind of touched him with memories of his dad and mother and his childhood with Ben. He went on to listening to Scootie some more then, smiling at her now and again and really showing some interest.

He asked a few questions as to just about how they'd planned to renew the old place, and as many grazing cattle begin to be seen in little mountain meadows and his attention was now drawed to them he started closing up on the subject by telling Scootie and Kip that he would think it over, and he would see what he could do so they could go ahead with their plans.

That went for about as good as a consent with the kids, and if pleased looks backed with thanks and gratefulness ever showed on any one's faces, none ever done any better showing than it did on the kids!

Then, when Kip finally could speak, he says, "I won't be a pumpkin kid all the time, Uncle Frank. Some day I'll be a good enough hand so I can work for you and I'll sure repay you first thing."

"And when I graduate," Scootie added on, "I can keep books for you. That would be of some help, wouldn't it?"

"Sure, oh sure," grins Frank, "but I'm thinking you kids just want a place to play in now and that you'll tire of it soon as the newness wears off."

"Not me," says Kip, now mighty well able to speak; "I would like to fix up the place like it was my own and make it my main camp, or home. I'm not going to be a city man, and soon as I can get out of school I'm going to live there, or in just some such a place. So there you are, Uncle Frank, and some day I'm going to be in the cow business, just like yourself.

"Well, well," says Frank, not grinning now. "That sounds good and all right to me. And now," he asks, turning to the girl, "how about you, Scootie?"

Scootie smiled at him. "I haven't really thought as much or as far ahead on the subject as I see Kip has," she says. "It's different with a girl. But I don't care for the city either, and even tho I have no such definite plans as Kip has I'm sure that I'd be very happy to fix up my end of the old place and make it at least my summer camp, for I don't know how many years to come."

"That's good, too," says Frank, "and it sounds pretty sure for some time. But," he went on, halfways grinning, "How about The Catamount Mining Company enterprise? You would need a camp there if you struck it rich."

Both the kids laughed. "If we strike it rich," says Kip, "I'd still want to keep my main camp in the old place." Then, he went on, "I could afford an airplane to visit the mine once in a while. Chuck could stay there."

"Yes, Chuck could stay there," Scootie also laughed, "and I could fly over with Kip when necessary. But I would keep the books at my place in the old house."

Frank rubbed his grinning chin. "Humph," he grunted; "well I guess that's that. But, as I said before," he went on, "I'll think it over about the old place and let you know tomorrow—Now one or both of you had better ride over to join Uncle Bill. I just seen him top a raise below that point over yonder."

Kip and Scootie looked at one another and Kip understood by his sister's look that it was for him to go. So Kip went while Scootie rode along with Frank. But no more was said about the fixing up of the old place. It was cattle to look after now and being that Scootie felt more relieved she enjoyed riding thru 'em as ever before.

So did Kip as he caught up and surprised Uncle Bill by again riding with him. Kip kept mum as to what had gone on on account he wasn't so very sure how that would turn out as yet. But his happy and satisfied expressions gave him away, and the wise Uncle Bill felt sure that something important had been gone over with Frank, and Frank had given in to whatever it was, as usual.

Uncle Bill didn't ask what it was, for he knew he'd soon enough find out, and he rode along at locating the bulls, happy to have one of the kids ride with him again and to see that he hadn't been deserted for no reason.

He found out what had been going on that evening, when Frank came down to confab with him at the bunk house. Frank told him of the kids' plans, and being that he figured Uncle Bill would know something about it he asked him what he thought on the subject. The old cowboy didn't hesitate in saying how he thought it was a mighty good plan and knew it would sure make the kids happy if they could go thru with it.

"I remember looking thru some of Martha's magazines last winter," he says, "and how schools had regular classes where kids was teached how to do different things so they wouldn't be so doggone helpless in doing odd jobs when they got out. It

He found out what had been going on that evening.

showed where they done carpentering work like benches, shelves and other handy things. The girls done other things for inside the house, and I got to thinking, ever since the kids started to get busy on the old place last summer that they'd sure learn a lot more at fixing up the old place, if they had the stuff to work with, and being they're so interested they'd sure have a lot of fun too, a lot of fun at learning to do something worth while doing. Yep," he wound up; "I sure agree to their plans and I know they'll work them thru."

"I see," says Frank, "and putting it the way you just did is something I didn't think of. You know," he grinned, "I don't go rummaging around in Martha's magazines, and so I'm not hep to all the stuff you been reading. But," he went on, now serious, "the way I had it figured I already thought it was a good plan anyhow. Seeing the old place going to ruin and into the ground always sort of reminded me of a neglected grave, and feeling ashamed for letting it go that way I've been riding around it. I didn't have the heart to burn it down as some folks do with sacred things, and I never got around to keep it up in shape. So, when the kids asked me about fixing up the place their own selves it set me to thinking right away that that would be a fine thing. I would be helping 'em with furnishing the stuff to do it with, which would sort of clear my conscience, they'd have a lot of fun at the work, and besides, being they're my own father and mother's grand children they have about as much right to living in there and do as they choose as my own children would, which I haven't got.

"Yep, Bill," he went on, "and I think my own argument is still stronger than yours, on the same idea too, and I know that we're both right. So the old house will have some more life and laughter about it again."

That decided on, it wasn't long for the kids to get wind of it. A word in Martha's ear and the good news was soon carried to them, before they started to go to bed, and which didn't at all help in putting 'em to sleep.

But they was up and ready for the regular and early breakfast time the next morning, and when Frank came to sit at the table with 'em they both felt sort of fidgety, for they wasn't supposed to know. They would let Frank take the lead on the subject, they figured, but it seemed to be taking him a long time starting in. In the meantime what little conversation went on was by jerks and not at all free and natural.

Finally Frank had to grin at their suspense, then he made up for that in a few quick words, saying, "Well, kids, you win. The work you two planned will go on, and starting today you'll have all the help and things you need to go on with.

"But," he went on, right at their happy faces and while they still couldn't say a word, "you two will have to do most of the work. I'll furnish you with men and teams to get the logs you need, have 'em set 'em up for you and do the heavy lifting when there's some to be done, but that's all and you two will have to do the rest to the finish. Do you want to do that?"

Their answer was better than Frank could ever expected. It was just what they wanted to do, they said, and had been afraid that he would have the men do that work for them. Now their cup of happiness was away over brimful.

"You know where the lumber pile and tool shop is," he went on, after the kids got thru talking. "Well, help yourselves there but take care of the tools and of not losing any. Come to think of it, I'll have Nick pick some out for you (Nick was the handy man, all around carpenter, blacksmith and good at most everything) and you can keep them at the place. Your ranch," he grinned. "He'll also help you with picking out the lumber, nails and such like, he'll find you some doors and windows stored away that you can use, and everything else you'll need. All you'll have to do is the work and do it well."

With that, all as they wished it to be and nothing to hold 'em back, they wasn't much for going on with eating their usual good breakfast that morning. They chopped it off pretty short, and when Martha, noticing their rush, told 'em it would be a long time till noon, they could only smile at her as they got up from the table, and then at their Uncle Frank for leaving him to finish his breakfast alone. He'd understand.

Frank well understood, and after they run out he looked at Martha and laughed. "Well," he says, "it looks like the old place is going to get the fixings, trimmings, and brushing up of its life starting right 'now.'"

CHAPTER ELEVEN

A S WITH MOST BIG RANCHES, the Five Barb always kept a good supply of new lumber on hand, also some old from camps and other buildings tore down to sometimes be built up in other places, all such is part of a ranch's equipment.

Kip and Scootie went to looking over the lumber and was well satisfied that all and whatever kind they'd need was in the neatly layed piles. Then to one side of the lumber was many big logs of all sizes and lengths, from over a foot thru down to long and straight lodge pine poles. Just right for a nice pole fence, also a light corral.

All hands was still in the cook house and eating while the kids went to rummaging around and finding things they'd need. Queer, they thought, they'd never noticed all the stuff before, but they hadn't thought of building then. They moseyed around and into the blacksmith, tool and carpenter shop, all in one good sized one room stone building, and they was looking over some tools when Nick walked in on 'em.

"Hello," he says, kind of gruff, but he wasn't gruff as he sounded, even if he was right particular as to who touched the tools. He done the handling of 'em.

"Frank just told me you'd want a few tools," he went on, "and for me to pick some out for you. Tell me what you want them for and I'll get 'em."

Then later, Frank came along with two ranch hands, and logs was picked out. The kids knew the length and size they'd need, and about how many. As for the lumber they wouldn't need that for some time, nor the ready made doors and windows they seen stored away. It would be some time before they'd want the poles too, and being they didn't know exactly what all they'd want right then they could always get it as they went along with their work and at the time it was needed.

To begin with they would have the logs hauled over, and being so big, long and heavy there'd have to be two loads made of 'em, even if it was a short and easy haul. There was two kant hooks brought along with the first load for the kids to roll the logs over with, for the bark was still on the logs and would have to be peeled before being used in the building.

It took the two men only about an hour to haul and unload the logs at the old place, and then they went on at their other ranch work, but it would take the kids at least two days to peel the bark off. That was *their* part of the job, like with any part of it they could possibly do. So, with each a draw knife and astraddle a log they went to their work, as happy as the larks that sang in the big trees around 'em.

Uncle Bill rode in on 'em as they was well started and going right on making the bark fly. "Howdy neighbors," he grins at 'em, like a friendly stranger, "I didn't know there was any new settlers come in these here parts. I see by the new timber you're peeling you ain't been here long."

141

That was their part of the job.

"No," says Kip, acting the pioneer. "Me and Mirandy, here," he pointed at Scootie, "we just pulled the harness off our horses in this spot come last full of the moon."

"But where are your horses?" asks Uncle Bill. "You know it's mighty unhandy besides being unhealthy to be afoot in this here wild country. Indians might drop in on you for your scalp most any time and run off with your horses if you don't keep 'em close."

"I have no fear," says Kip, patting a kant hook like it was his trusty rifle, "Old Betsy here will make the Indians bite the dust before they could get to our horses or our scalp."

"Well, well, you're a brave man," says Uncle Bill, admiring, "and what might be your name, pardner?"

Kip had to think for a spell, then looking his fiercest, he says, "I'm known thru the Indian territory as Hawkeye Hogan, the Indian fighter."

Uncle Bill whistled, as in great surprise. "Not the Hawkeye who outfit General Seemore in the wicked Comanpatches battle, be you?"

"None other, sir," proudly answers Kip, and then, "What might be your name?" he asks.

"Me," humbly answers Uncle Bill, "why, I'm known as Horntoad Ratburn in the trapping country. I trap butterflies and gather snake eyelashes."

The play acting and talk turned to the work of the day and the start that was being made. Uncle Bill got off his horse and went to looking the logs over. "Ought to make dandy ridge logs," he says, "plenty big and long, and straight too. Frank just had 'em cut last year, must of had a hunch of you kids wanting 'em."

"Maybe," says Kip. Then wondering, "Maybe he did have a hunch, and more than that if he happened to ride by here and noticed the work we'd done on the place. Come to think of it," he went on, "he did say, just yesterday, that he'd noticed the work we'd done here."

"He's a foxy scamper," says Uncle Bill, "and maybe he wouldn't let on he was interested or had any idea of what you kids was up to, just to see what you two would do and have some fun with you. I don't know of any place where he'd have use for them logs this year. But I can't understand why he didn't have 'em peeled when they was cut and the sap was up. He always did."

"I think I understand," says Kip, grinning. "That's our job and he had it left on for *us* to peel."

"Maybe you're right. . . . Anyhow, you sure have plenty of stuff and everything to work with, your Uncle Frank will see to that."

"Yes," says Scootie, smiling, "and thanks to you too."

The old cowboy looked at her, all surprise. "Thanks to me, why?"

"Why, fish hooks," says Kip, "our suspicions are well founded and grounded. . . . Who was it," he went on to ask, "told Martha it was all decided, that it was all fixed and we would have all we wanted for us to go ahead with our plans on this place? Answer us that."

Uncle Bill fidgeted some, plucked at a weed and then grinning under his hat brim, he answered, "It was Frank brought the subject up to me," he says. "I only said the idea was all right."

"Yes, sure," says Kip, "and I suppose that was all—"

"But we'll forgive you, Uncle Bill," Scootie joins in, smiling, "and we're certainly very thankful and happy."

The old cowboy stood up, he couldn't stand any show of gratitude. He fidgeted, brushing the dirt off his weathered leather shaps careful as tho they was of full dress broadcloth, then turned to get on his horse.

"Well, you got a big job on your hands, Kids," he says, as he slipped into the saddle to ride away, "and I hope it will all be a lot of fun."

"It sure will, Uncle Bill," says Kip.

The old cowboy rode away, chuckling to himself and mighty pleased with everything in general. He of course now seen that he wouldn't get much of the kids' company for some time to come because it would take them the biggest part of the summer to fix up the old house and get moved in right, as they planned to do. But there was a lot of hard riding cut out for him that summer, the kind of riding he could do better without the kids, so that all balanced well to make things all right in every way.

There would come times when there'd be some riding that'd be of more than average interest for the kids and when they could even be of some help, but they was so much more interested and hard at their work that riding only come second now. The one long ride they kept a looking forward to, thought of and talked about as they worked was the one back to The Basin, to get the mountain lions and finish exploring the tunnel and shaft. It would sure be fun with Uncle Bill and Chuck, and for that ride they would be ready to stop work, put away their tools and saddle up quick, any time the word was given.

But the trip back to The Basin would be delayed some, on account that Chuck was now at a line camp up on the mountain and would have to stay there longer than was expected. It was a busy time. Round up was started, a few of Frank's cowboys rode in from different line camps and was sent to "rep" (represent) the Five Barb with neighboring outfits that was combing the ranges of all cattle, and to drive back to the home range all cattle that'd strayed during the winter before. Then the round up and branding on home ranges would follow on.

Frank had to line some more cowboys for the work, which started from spring round up, on to the shifting of the cattle to different ranges, afterwards the horse round up with the branding of the colts and the cutting out of geldings to be broke and others to be shipped and sold, then to riding line again with keeping the cattle from straying, and that work goes till fall round up, another branding of late spring calves, and on till beef round up and trailing to the shipping point. The end of the season's work, when some of the cowboys are let go and some drift on to other ranges for winter work, where in some countries it goes on the year around.

Kip and Scootie would of sure liked to went along when the cowboys rode in. Saddle horses was run in from the range and all prepared to go on round up, but their work on the old place still had the strongest holt and they stayed at it. With that, they was expecting Chuck to ride down from his line camp most any time now and ready for the trip to The Basin. They would miss being with the round up but they didn't mind that so much because they could see one again some other time, but not often with the lion hunting nor the mine exploring.

So, along with their work they was satisfied to stay and look forward to that. There was only about a day all together when they didn't work, so as to see the frisky saddle horses brought in from the range after a long winter's freedom and rest all slick and fat and full of snorts. Even some of the old cow horses made their riders pay close attention to their riding, and of course the kids had to be close to see them topped off.

They always enjoyed the gathering of the many horses, and watching the separating of the ones that was wanted from the ones that wasn't, and being the kids wasn't going to be on the cattle round up they cheered themselves to think that they'd sure be on the horse round up afterwards. They'd have the house about

*Even some of the old cow horses made their riders
pay close attention to their riding.*

done by then, and in the meantime they'd sure have their hands full, and some excitement too with the trip to The Basin.

Frank and his riders with their strings of saddle horses rode away, leaving the ranch with only two riders for the time, Uncle Bill, now taking Frank's place as all around foreman, and Mac helping along with the riding. Kip and Scootie was now done with the peeling of the logs, raked the pitchy bark up in a pile for good kindling when a fire might be needed later on, and then a couple of ranch hands and Nick rolled the heavy logs up to the roof, notched and fitted 'em, and soon enough the heavy ridge logs was rolled up to the top of them to fit mighty solid.

The kids was like squirrels in running around in doing all they could to help, and with the long ridge logs now up and the house taking shape, about all they could do was jump up and down in one place in their happiness.

But soon there now come a couple of wagon loads of lumber to be nailed on for the start of the roof and that held 'em down to work some more. That was something *they* could do, and the ranch hands left 'em again to go on with their other work. Nick stayed for a while to get the kids started right with laying the long boards, and then he also left 'em to their pleasure.

The boards was nailed on well and careful in about a day, and then Nick was called on again. Two square holes would have to be cut in the roof for a chimney, one in each cabin roof, and after the kids decided where they'd each want their stove that was done, with Nick's coaching.

Then tar paper was spread on the boards, and on top of that, long and wide sheets of galvanized, corrugated iron was laid and to cover the whole roof. Two more holes had to be cut into that for the chimneys, and then the chimneys, made out of square five-gallon kerosene cans, was put in. A big round hole had been cut in the bottom of each can, a length of stove pipe fitted thru and then dirt put in the space that was between the can and the pipe to keep the heat of the stove pipe from getting to the roofing.

Nick had to do most of the work at laying the paper and corrugated iron and fitting the chimneys. He also fitted and fastened the five-inch holes around and on the edge of the roof, which would be the thickness of the shale dirt levelled over the corrugated iron, the ranch hands would do the hauling and shovelling of the shale, and that would finish the roof, a solid six inches of thickness that would be sure to keep out the cold as well as the heat and would easy last a long lifetime.

Another pretty sight for the kids to see done, and while that was being done the flooring was started. Nick of course had to fit the stringers there, for that was no beginner's job, neither was the laying of the first floor boards. But it made it easier that the boards was of twelve-inch width and not the regular narrow flooring, and after the first few was fitted, the kids went right on to doing the rest without Nick's help.

It hadn't been much to Nick's taste to be working with the kids, like at their job and as tho he was a kid playing too. But that was at first, and his natural gruffiness was even more gruffy then, until, as job after job was started and finished and the kids showed such good sense and ability at helping and working on when they could that he gradually lost most of his gruffiness, even to some of it that was his own nature. He even got to smiling, more and more often and sometimes loud enough so he could be heard as the kids passed remarks or made mistakes, something which the men at the ranch seldom seen him do. It'd been hard for the kids to get his help at first, when they'd needed him for a short spell, but it wasn't long when all they'd have to do was crook a finger and he'd come a running. He also got to stay longer than was necessary and to doing things the kids could and wanted to do themselves, just for the sake of being in their company. Then come a time when the kids would remind him of that fact when he started doing what they called their work, then he'd just grin, talk with 'em a spell and after a while pick up his tools and go back to his shop.

Uncle Bill rode in on him one time as he was a jabbering away to the kids and not seeming to be doing anything, while the kids was working, and that so surprised the old cowboy that he couldn't say a word for a spell, for Nick carrying a conversation with anybody, especially with the kids, and doing most of the talking was something mighty rare.

Getting off his horse and coming into the house, he was for sitting in on the conversation, but Nick soon stopped his talking, then, picked up his tools and went back to the shop again. The old cowboy laughed.

"I hope I haven't put out his fire," he says. "I never did see the old boy line out to talking the way he was when I rode in."

Then noticing the good work on laying the floor and how the kids was going at it to make the boards fit tight together, he went on to remark that with Nick's help they'd be carpenters and all around builders by the time they'd get thru with the house.

"Yes," says Kip, "and we need Nick's help to get started once in a while, so it's done right."

"Sure," Uncle Bill was quick to say, "and I would sure need some help too if I was to do any such work. . . . At the rate you kids are going you'll have the old homestead pretty well along by the time we go on our lion hunting and mine exploring trip. Chuck ought to be riding down from his mountain camp any day now."

Kip and Scootie stopped their hammering and perked their ears up at that. Both smiled with pleasure at the thought of the trip, and after some comments on it went back to their hammering.

"It'll sure be a lot of fun, all right," says Kip, with a wide grin, "and this is a lot of fun too."

Uncle Bill had rode in and visited with the kids a couple or three times a day as they went on with their work, and he was pleased to see how well they'd done and hadn't called for no help only when absolutely necessary. He'd also noticed that even with handy Nick they wouldn't let him do any of *their* work, what they was supposed to do themselves.

The flooring down, well fitted and nailed, the frame work for doors and windows was next to be done, and Nick was again called on to help there. Doors and windows that could be used was picked out from where they'd been stored away, fitted to the frame or the frame fitted to them. That was too careful a work for the kids to tackle by themselves, but they helped all they could, and when they couldn't they went to knocking out the old chinking[1] that was about to fall out from between the logs and replacing it new.

Nick had started 'em with that work, there was quite a bit of it to do inside and out, and when he seen they'd caught on and was doing well he went on with the frame, window and door fitting work, sometimes whistling or talking away to the kids as he did.

The good solid roof now on the old place which now begin to look new again, the floor well laid, the windows fitted and the doors hung the kids was fast going on with the chinking. The next work now would be the plastering, or "muddying up" between the logs, and with a little coaching from Nick to start in with as to how to mix the mortar of lime and sand and then to plastering it on the chinking with the trowel they could go right on with that job by themselves.

They could now go right on with all the other work without any more help from anybody. The inside finishing, such as shelves, trimmings, and other final decorating would of course be all of their own doings, so would be the painting of the floors, doors. and window frames.

Outside, and with the fence around the place, the round corral and small shed adjoining that would sure be all of their own doing too, the digging of post holes, tamping and all. They'd

---

[1]Chinking: Fitting and nailing long strips of wood between gaps in the logs, to fill in space and for plaster to hold to.

A right good home and main camp

only need to have the posts and poles hauled to them and they'd be happy to do the rest.

They was more free now with the feeling that they really was renewing the old place by theirselves, like they might be building a new one of their own, and when they put their tools away one evening, after a long day's work and only a little more chinking to do, they was pleased with the shelter of the good roof over their heads, the solid floor under their feet and the solidity and brightness of the whole building. It was a place where the heat of the sun, the dampness of the rains and the cold of winters and snows couldn't faze 'em, a right good home and main camp which they would finish and furnish to each their hearts content, with, as Kip put it, a roofed over and open fighting space in between.

Closing the doors of their place they started away for the ranch house. They'd got about half ways to it when, going thru a little clearing and happening to look beyond the corrals, they seen a rider driving a few horses and coming along there. The kids made a run for the corrals and to meet him, for they had a strong hunch as to who the rider was.

And their hunch was right. The rider was Chuck.

CHAPTER TWELVE

CHUCK'S RETURN TO THE RANCH meant only one thing for Kip and Scootie, the trip to The Basin. And there was no rest for them that evening he rode in, nor no rest for Chuck and Uncle Bill until the time for that trip was decided on and that to be made soon as possible.

Chuck didn't seem to be in no hurry about it, remarking that it'd take a little time to prepare for such a "wild adventure and dangerous trip," maybe a couple of days. Then Uncle Bill acted like he wanted to renig and that there was no use of his going, adding on for excuse that he should stay with the ranch and do the riding that was to be done.

But the kids wasn't to be put off. They got to working on Chuck with the idea that the lions might be gone if he waited, that somebody else might beat him to 'em, and also find the gold that might be laying in the tunnel or shaft, just like waiting to be grabbed. That seemed to work on Chuck, for he acted kind of serious and worried and he finally had to remark, as he sneaked a wink to Uncle Bill, that they might be right.

Uncle Bill's shell was harder to crack. They had to remind him of how their Uncle Frank had "appointed him as overseer for the trip, also to act in the capacity of chief cook and bottle washer."

"Besides," Kip went on to say, "Mac can do all the riding there is to be done here for awhile. I know, because I heard Uncle Frank say so. . . . We won't be gone long, anyway."

Uncle Bill scratched his head, returned Chuck's wink, and finally said:

"Well, orders is orders, and I guess I'll have to go along and do as I was told. I'll be ready when Chuck is."

As Chuck had said he'd be ready in a couple of days, that settled it, and the kids went to sleep on it that night, satisfied. They was up early the next morning and doing their own preparing for the trip, but that didn't take 'em long, and as it was, Uncle Bill told 'em to leave behind over half of what they'd gathered.

"I don't think we'll be gone over a year," he says, grinning at what they'd gathered to take along. "All you'll need is a round-up bed made up of a couple of blankets, a couple of soogans and a tarp, then stuff in one change of clothes, that's all and enough for all summer. We don't want to trail a whole string of pack horses with us, we're taking only two, one for the bedding and the other for the grub."

The kids cut the pack down a considerable at that, but they kept one thing which they thought would be extra, and that was a strong flashlight which they'd brought with 'em from the East. They'd never seen Uncle Bill nor any of the cowboys use one, but they figured that it would come in mighty handy, and even necessary in exploring the tunnel and shaft. They well remembered how they'd wished they had it the first time they was in there.

Being all set and everything ready for the trip long before that noon they then went to their house which, as they got near, looked mighty homey and inviting. They would of liked mighty well to've gone on with their work there, and for a while it was a toss up as to whether they'd rather stay and do that or go on with the trip. But, as they finally got to thinking, the house would keep, mighty well and for a long time, and would sure be there to welcome 'em when they got back. That wouldn't be the case with the lions, even if the tunnel would keep, so, deciding on the trip and cheering themselves up with the thought that they could go right on with the place again when they'd get back they took another look around inside, seen that the tools was well put away and then they went out, making sure of closing the doors tight and to stay against whatever wind or storm might come.

Feeling secure about their place, and now anxious to get on with the trip, they would see as to what they could do to crowd the starting some. Chuck and Mac had gone out riding early that morning, and Uncle Bill had also went some time later. He come back a little before noon and driving a few cattle, which he corralled. The kids was right there as he did, and watched while he cut out a fine, fat but odd colored yearling that was to be kept in the corral. Then he let the others out to go on back to their range. At that the kids wanted to know why that one was kept in.

"Just one of Chuck's ideas which your Uncle Frank agreed to," says the old cowboy. "We're going to butcher it this evening when it gets cool, then keep one half here for the ranch and take the other half to the Morrisons' to sort of even up for the favor

*He cut out a fine, fat but odd colored yearling
that was to be kept in the corral.*

they done us. The other parts, such as the head and some of the insides, will be used for lion bait."

"It'll sure be well divided up and come in handy all around, won't it?" says Kip.

"Yes," says Scootie, "but it seems a shame to kill such a pretty animal."

"Sure," Uncle Bill adds on, "us humans ain't any better than lions that way."

When Chuck also rode in that noon and all was thru eating, the kids started from there on to rushing the start of the trip. They brought up and imagined many reasons why there should be no delay, and as neither Chuck nor Uncle Bill went riding that afternoon on account of getting things together and ready for the trip, they had to listen to all their reasons for the rush.

The afternoon wore on with the kids following 'em around that way, and then, as Chuck had the pack riggings about ready he put a sudden end to their making up more reasons.

"All right," he says, like he'd figured it out with 'em as they'd talked. "Be ready for breakfast at four tomorrow morning, and we'll start out right away after."

"Good idea," grins Uncle Bill, "and it'll give Chuck more time at the Morrisons', too, which'll be nice."

"Yeh," says Chuck, not at all set back at the remark. "I was thinking of the beef we'll be butchering this evening too, of the fresh meat not souring and starting to spoil on the way. If we start early in the morning we'll be in the cool of the timber till near noon, then we can stop at the edge of it during the heat of the day, cross the plain in the afternoon, and get to Morrisons' a little after dark. That'll be a good day's ride and we can easy make it to Rock Creek and near The Basin day after tomorrow."

"I'll have to admit you're figuring right," says Uncle Bill, "even to making sure of not missing the stop at Morrisons', which is taking us out of our way some. But it's worth it."

"You bet," grins Chuck, "So was the stuff we borrowed from 'em."

It was barely daybreak as Chuck corralled the horses the next morning, while Uncle Bill hollered to get the sleepy kids up and see they got ready. The horses was saddled and packed in the dim first light of day, breakfast was gone thru in a short time, and Martha having fixed a special good lunch for the four bid 'em good bye, warning the kids to "be careful now."

The outfit strung out, Uncle Bill and Chuck each leading a pack horse, and the kids left to ride as they pleased. Good time was made, and the day being cooler than the ones before made the travelling more to all's liking. Maybe that accounted for fewer arguments between the old and younger cowboy along the way that day, and when the Morrison ranch was reached a little after dark that evening there was an open welcome there that made the kids feel as much as in their own home.

There was no outside cooking, as Chuck and Uncle Bill had figured on doing when they got there, for while they argued with Pop Morrison about it the ladies went on to set the table, not at all paying any attention to their arguing, and that settled it.

But the four travellers wasn't going to be argued out of sleeping outside. The kids both chipped in a few words as to that, and after a mighty good supper and as pleasant an evening they all filed out to where they'd spread their beds, in one corner of the big lawn and around a big tree, where the half of the beef was hung high for the cool of the night.

Two of the four travellers went to sleep soon as they hit their soogans that night, they was Uncle Bill and Kip. The other two layed awake for a spell, Chuck with thinking of Julie and for what a great girl she was, and Scootie with thinking of Julie too, and what a surprise she'd got at meeting her. She'd halfways expected to see a kind of rough, back-country-like sort of a girl, a little ignorant and bashful, or else a flashy loud kind like she'd seen in "Wild and woolly west" posters and such. But here she'd come to see a perfect-at-ease and pretty young lady, only a couple of years older than herself, with pleasant smile and manners that'd put many a girl she knew to shame. Scootie liked her the minute she met her, and it was the same with Julie for Scootie.

Uncle Bill was the first one up the next morning, as usual and at daybreak. Chuck was close second, and the two right away went to smuggle the half a beef they'd brought into the ice house, so as nobody would know about it until after they got away. For they didn't want to hear no words of thanks.

They didn't get that done any too soon, and they'd just got back to wake the kids up when Pop Morrison come up on 'em. He'd already been down to the corrals. The three squatted down on the grass and smoked and talked while the kids scrambled out of their beds. The squeak of a corral gate meant the horses had been brought in. Then soon after the big triangle iron at the ranch house was rung, breakfast was ready, and a new day was started.

The parting that followed the easy talk thru and after the good breakfast was of the kind that went with the openness of the country and the clearness of the sky. There was a standing welcome there that went with the four for whenever they would return.

As Chuck had figured, it was an easy ride to Rock Creek, and camp was set by the spring above the corral again, where they'd camped while holding the bulls and waited till the swollen creek went down after the cloudburst. On account of the grass and water for the horses there it was the best and closest camping place to the deserted mine.

Camp set and all having a bite to eat, Chuck was for going on to the tunnel that evening. He'd brought two bear traps and a few heavy wolf traps with the pack and he wanted to set them that evening, for during the night is when the lions would be doing their prowling, in and out. He was for going alone, but the kids now rested some there was no leaving them behind, and Uncle Bill, after debating with himself for a while, decided to go too, for, as he got to figuring, there was no telling what a she lion would do if she had some young ones there.

The dugout at the mouth of the tunnel was reached a little before sundown. "Just right," says Chuck as he got off his horse and tied him to the exact same juniper Kip and Scootie had tied theirs that first time. Then he took his traps and rifle, and Uncle

Bill the gunny sack of beef for the baiting, and also his rifle. The kids trailed along behind, their hearts a beating in fair shape, and when all got into the dark of the dugout and to the darker entrance of the tunnel is when Kip produced the flashlight he'd brought along.

"Thought it'd come in handy," he says as he turned it on.

"It sure will," says Chuck, surprised and then pleased. "Kind of dark in this tunnel."

He dropped his traps at the entrance, then keeping his rifle and taking the flashlight from Kip, he went on to say: "There's no use of setting the traps until we know there's lions here." He held the light to the ground. "I see fresh tracks but I'll go in and make sure if there's some inside. Bill," he grinned, "you stay here with the kids and count 'em as they come out."

"All right," the old cowboy grinned back at him, "but don't you be a yowling when you come out yourself or I might take you for a lion." Saying that, he levered a cartridge into his rifle barrel. Then turning to the kids. "Do you two want to go in with Chuck?" he asks, not meaning it.

"N-n-n-o, no," says Scootie, frightened just at the thought.

"N-nor me either," Kip also said. Then he grinned a little, "I'll wait awhile."

The two backed to one side and well away from the entrance, behind Uncle Bill, and Chuck started on into the tunnel, there to be near knocked down by the swarm of bats as the strong ray of the flashlight went along it. He'd forgot about them, but getting closer to the ground he went on, well noticing then how the tunnel floor was about covered with lion tracks.

He was glad to have the flashlight and he shot it along the tunnel as he went, but as there was a turn in it the light couldn't reach very far. Then he come to a hole about the width of the tunnel. It must be the shaft Kip and Scootie had fell into, he thought, and he'd just turned his light and got a glance of the skeleton at the bottom when he heard low, but mighty threatening growls which echoed and carried on thru the tunnel, even to the ears of Uncle Bill and the kids.

Chuck, raising his flashlight to the sound, felt a shiver along his spine, for, from the light there reflected two pairs of glaring eyes. He was sure of two pairs, but thinking there might be more, and now over his first scare he kept his light on the eyes, the low, warning growls went on the while he figured of some way of getting 'em there and then. He thought of firing at 'em from where he was, but he wouldn't be sure of his aim on account he couldn't get to see his sights very well, and he'd be in a kind of a narrow place in case he just crippled one or the other, or others, and they come for or past him to get out.

He thought too of piling in brush and smoking them out, first setting the traps at the entrance and shooting the ones that might escape them, but that would be a lot of work and take a lot of time. Then the shaft would be quite some handicap, too.

Then the thought of the shaft gave him an idea. He went back to the entrance to warn Uncle Bill to get ready for any lions coming out, that he was going to shoot 'em out, and before the old cowboy could say a word, Chuck had went back into the tunnel.

Being anxious, there was "no time like the present," he thought, and "when there's a will there's a way," he also thought, as he got back to the shaft. Setting the flashlight where it couldn't fall and so he could see good, and while the threatening growls was going on again, only louder, he loosened a couple of the timbers that was still left on top of the shaft and slid 'em to the bottom. Then, with his rifle, he slid down after 'em.

Down there, trying not to step on the skeleton, he propped the timbers against the other side of the shaft, and having a great advantage over the kids in being taller, also with the light, he soon got his head and elbows over the edge, his rifle in his hands, and from the light he could now well enough see his sights, also, the two pairs of glaring eyes at the end of the tunnel.

He aimed carefully between one pair of two glaring eyes and fired. That first shot, in the narrow tunnel, sounded like the earth itself might be exploded. Echoing with that came an unearthly sounding scream, along with a flood-like swarm of bats, stirred dust, and powder smoke.

Chuck near lost his perch for a second at all the goings on, and a second later he did lose it, as he fired another shot at another lion coming mighty fast and like right for him. But the scared and mad lion, confused by the blinding light from acrost the shaft, went straight for it instead and half knocked Chuck off his perch as he did. Chuck done the other half and went on down to the bottom, to get out of the lion's way, and so he'd clear the shaft opening, for, as he said afterwards, it would of been kind of in close quarters for him and that lion in the bottom of that shaft.

As the lion cleared the shaft on his way out he knocked the flashlight from where Chuck had set it on top, scaring the lion all the more and now leaving Chuck in the dark. The lion then made for the entrance of the tunnel like all the spooks inside the earth was after him, near with the speed of a bullet, and his aim was good for the outside entrance. But Uncle Bill's aim in the dugout was still better, and shooting at such close range stopped the lion to do his death scream and struggle right at the entrance.

The kids was petrified with fear at the sight, the deafening roar of the shot and the scream of the lion. They got their thrill of the day for a long time to come in just a few seconds, and they wasn't wanting any more. But Uncle Bill shot again, to make sure of the lion, which then lay limp.

The echoes of the shots and screams died down and then all was quiet again, quiet and dark as a tomb. But not for so long, another echo with the sound of Chuck's voice was heard. After a while the ray of his flashlight was seen coming out of the tunnel, and then he come to sight.

"Sure had to do some tall scrambling to get out of the old shaft," he says, "but that old shaft sure came in handy." Then seeing the dead lion at the entrance of the tunnel: "I see you got my pet," he went on. "Yeh, he patted me on the head as he went over me. I've got his mate at the end of the tunnel, she's deader than a door nailed, and I believe I hit this one too, even if I did have to shoot mighty quick."

Him and Uncle Bill went to investigate, and the kids, now over their scare, was able to move and follow. It was seen that Chuck's

But Uncle Bill's aim in the dugout was still better.

bullet had sure enough hit the lion, right thru the shoulder and above the heart and even tho he'd soon died it wasn't a shot to stop him quick. Uncle Bill had put the quick finishing touch there.

Being sure there was no more lions in the tunnel, Chuck went to setting all the traps he had anyway, remarking that there might be some come from the outside to water at the head of the tunnel, where the other lion lay dead. The bait of beef was scattered from the inside of the tunnel on out, the dead lion at the entrance was drug away out of scent and to be skinned along with the other the next morning, when the traps would be looked at and the tunnel would be explored.

It was good and dark as the four hunters, very pleased with that day's kill, started back for their camp. A good meal was cooked while the events of the day was talked over, then they soon rolled into their blankets, and like as tho the sun had no more than gone down it was daybreak and up again. Another day, and maybe some more lions.

A good breakfast of plenty of hot coffee, fried beef, and pan bread, and the four riders was in the saddle again, with not much hopes of getting any more lions this day. But if not, the kids figured the good exploring of the tunnel and shaft would make up for that.

They'd rode along at a good gait, and was to about half a mile of the mine when Uncle Bill pulled his horse to a stop and pointed down to the trail.

"Look-see here," he says. "Another big cat has gone to the tunnel, and since we left there last night, too."

The kids rode close to where Uncle Bill was pointing. They looked but they couldn't see the track, then Uncle Bill got off his horse and with a brush twig outlined the whole print of the padded foot in the gravelly ground. It wasn't very plain but a little further on he showed 'em another which was plainer.

"But how can you tell," asks Scootie, in wonder, "that the big cat passed here since we left last night?"

"Why, that's easy," says Uncle Bill. "You can see where the lion's tracks are over the tracks our horses made in going to camp last night, and that being the case shows that the lion passed since our horses did."

"Yes," says Chuck, as all proceeded on, "and I hope he went in the tunnel and got into one of the traps."

Chuck well got his wish, for at the tunnel he seen where the big cat didn't get into only one of the traps but, in his fighting to get loose, got in two of 'em.

"Well, that aint bad," he says to Uncle Bill, as he aimed his rifle at the snarling lion and pulled the trigger. "One more lion now and we'll have one apiece."

The lions was drug out and hung to junipers, all hands went to skinning, and with the kids each helping under the coaching of Uncle Bill and Chuck it didn't take long to do the work.

"These skins will look good hanging up on the walls of your ranch house," says Chuck to the kids as the last lion was skinned.

"They look better on the lions," says Scootie, "if they wasn't so mean."

"But let's do some exploring now," says Kip, anxious, now that the skinning was done, "and see if we can find some gold."

169

That being agreeable the three of The Catamount Mining Company went back to the entrance of the tunnel, picked up different old tools that'd been there and started on their exploring, Chuck taking the lead with the flashlight, and Uncle Bill trailing along behind, like to just get one look at the tunnel and not with any thought of looking for gold.

The shaft was the first place looked into. Chuck and Kip went down, while Uncle Bill and Scootie watched 'em from above. The skeleton bones was carefully picked up, looked at one by one for some kind of clue and stacked away in one corner. Then Kip picked up one, a part of a center rib, and Uncle Bill spoke for a look at it. The other part of the rib was found and both pieces was throwed up to him.

"Just as I thought," he says, as he put the pieces together. "As neat a shatter of a bullet hole as anybody'd want to see, and right where it'd do the most damage. And now, Mr. Chuck," he went on, "don't that show that the man was killed and what for? . . . The shaft being covered also proves that too, don't it?"

"Yes, I guess it does," Chuck had to admit, "but that ain't no reason why there can't be more gold here besides what the prospector found."

"It ain't likely there is," says Uncle Bill, as final, "or there'd been some more digging done."

Not being discouraged any, Chuck grinned up at him. "All right, you old wet blanket," he says, and went back to his work. About then Kip found one more nugget, awhile later Chuck found two, and grinning all the more, there was some exciting digging and scratching from then on, deep and wide.

But even tho they worked and sweated for a couple of hours in the small space, not another nugget was found. In the meantime, like tired of watching and sure that no more would be found, Uncle Bill had disappeared, and when Chuck and Kip came out of the shaft, hollered for him and they heard his answer, it came from the far end of the tunnel, by the spring there.

Helping Scootie acrost the shaft the three went to where the old cowboy was squatted and lighting matches by where a little trickle of water, about half the size of a 30-30 cartridge, oozed out of a crack in the rock and sank a few feet away. As the three came near, Uncle Bill looked up, held out his hand and by the flashlight he showed 'em about half a dozen nuggets averaging well to the size of buckshot.

"What gold's been found in these diggings," says the old cowboy to the three very surprised faces, "has been by following this little trickle here," meaning the spring. "It most likely was only a seepage covered with rye grass when the prospector started digging. This little trickle here might of been a big river some thousands and thousands of years ago, coming from big glaciers, washing these nuggets from the earth and leaving little deposits like we've already found.

"Yessir, by golly," says Chuck, as pleased as the kids, "and by digging along this trickle a feller might find some pretty good pockets and deposits of these nuggets. Maybe get into a regular underground stream or river, like some has been found and where there might be some *big* gold deposits."

"Mebbe so," says Uncle Bill. "There's a lot of digging between this spot and the bowels of the earth that's not taken up," he grinned, "and a feller can never tell what might be found from here to there and on thru till you come out in China. Finding pockets of gold is not at all sure, you know that. A feller might dig on just a few feet from here and find a fortune, but it's a heap more likely that a whole fortune might be spent in digging on and on and not finding another nugget. By the formations of the rock and the way the water is running I'm thinking we've found all the gold there is here. If there was any more you can bet your boots there'd be a mining camp right on the spot and we wouldn't be sitting where we are."

But even with the old cowboy's talk, which Chuck figured was plenty true and was sure enough a gamble, he wasn't for leaving without some try at finding more nuggets. Kip and Scootie both well agreed to that too, and so, with what was left of a pick, Chuck went to work along where the water was trickling out, while the kids pounded the earth and rock he dug out, all excited in looking for more nuggets. Uncle Bill only sat back on a rock, held the flashlight to their best advantage, and smiled.

The three worked on till quite a hole was added on to the tunnel, the dirt pounded, scratched over and scraped back, and not another nugget was found. Uncle Bill thought it was a good thing they didn't or they might of worked themselves sick. As it was, the resting spells begin to come more and more often, and being they hadn't brought no lunch the stomachs got to growling their hunger and the thoughts of juicy steaks got juicier, replacing the visions of cold hard nuggets.

It was middle afternoon when they decided to quit for the day, with Chuck remarking that he could of done a lot better if he'd had the tools to work with. But he would dig at it some more on the next day, and to make the coming more worth while he set the traps again, hoping to catch another lion during the night.

But not a track showed when the four rode to the tunnel again the next morning, and the only trap sprung was by a magpie which, like a finish to the whole thing, was squawking its loudest.

"Looks like we've played out our string," says Uncle Bill, "on lions and gold, both."

"Yep," grins Chuck, "and you can have the magpie."

But the good night's rest had sort of freshened and renewed Chuck's and the kids' hopes of finding a pocket of nuggets, or at least one. They'd brought something for lunch that day too and was prepared for a good stay at the digging. So the three went at it like as tho they meant it again, while Uncle Bill took on his position of throwing light on the work.

It was long before noon time when the spirit of the three gold seekers begin to dwindle a considerable. The lunch was et up before it was time for it to be, and then, with the excuse of making sure if there was any more lions around, Chuck said he'd make a little circle looking for tracks and signs of 'em and got on his horse and rode away, leaving the kids with Uncle Bill and to do all the digging they wished. He would be back to work on with 'em sometime in the afternoon.

All the digging the kids done that afternoon wouldn't of filled a bucket. They scratched half hearted at what dirt had already been dug out, and finally Scootie dropped the short drill she'd used. Kip grinned at Uncle Bill and doing the same as Scootie had, he remarked.

"And I think Chuck had better pick up his traps, too."

It was at The Gap the next afternoon as four riders topped a high ridge of mountains when, before going on to drop down on the Five Barb range, one of the riders looked back at the country now left behind, waved a hand and remarked:

"I still feel 'thar's gold in them thar hills,—'" that rider grinned,—"and I'm going back there some day again and dig some more for it."

"Yep," says another rider, "and spend all you earn or find putting it back into the ground to looking for more, like most all desert rats do."

The other two and younger riders only smiled at the talk but didn't look back for another look-see. For now well pleased with the outcome of the trip to "them thar hills" they was also glad to return, and their minds was now on the log house amongst the big cottonwoods in the valley ahead. Their main camp and ranch to complete.

WILL JAMES was born Joseph Ernest Nephtali Dufault in the province of Quebec on June 6, 1892. He left home as a teenager to live out his dream of becoming a cowboy in the American West. James went on to write and illustrate twenty-four books and numerous magazine articles about horses, cowboying, and the West. His works soon captured the imagination of the public. He died in 1942, at the age of fifty.

We encourage you to patronize your local bookstore. Most stores will order any title that they do not stock. You may also order directly from Mountain Press using the order form provided below or by calling our toll-free number and using your credit card.

Other fine Will James Titles:

_____ Cowboys North and South	14.00/paper	25.00/cloth
_____ The Drifting Cowboy	14.00/paper	25.00/cloth
_____ Smoky, the Cowhorse	16.00/paper	36.00/cloth
_____ Cow Country	14.00/paper	25.00/cloth
_____ Sand	16.00/paper	30.00/cloth
_____ Lone Cowboy	16.00/paper	30.00/cloth
_____ Sun Up	16.00/paper	30.00/cloth
_____ Big-Enough	16.00/paper	30.00/cloth
_____ Uncle Bill	14.00/paper	26.00/cloth
_____ All in the Day's Riding	16.00/paper	30.00/cloth
_____ The Three Mustangeers	15.00/paper	30.00/cloth
_____ Home Ranch	16.00/paper	30.00/cloth
_____ Young Cowboy		15.00/cloth
_____ In the Saddle with Uncle Bill	14.00/paper	26.00/cloth
_____ Scorpion, A Good Bad Horse	15.00/paper	30.00/cloth
_____ Flint Spears, Cowboy Rodeo Contestant	15.00/paper	30.00/cloth
_____ Cowboy in the Making		15.00/cloth
_____ Look-See with Uncle Bill	14.00/paper	26.00/cloth
_____ Ride for the High Points: _The Real Story of Will James_ (Jim Bramlett)	20.00/paper	
_____ The Will James Books: _A Descriptive Bibliography for Enthusiasts and Collectors_ (Don Frazier)	18.00/paper	

Please include $3.00 per order to cover postage and handling.

Please send the books marked above. I have enclosed $ _____

Name _____

Address _____

City/State/Zip _____

☐ Payment enclosed (check or money order in U.S. funds)

Bill my: ☐ VISA ☐ MasterCard ☐ Discover ☐ American Express

Card No. _____ Exp. Date _____

Signature _____

MOUNTAIN PRESS PUBLISHING COMPANY
Post Office Box 2399 • Missoula, Montana 59806
Order Toll-Free **1-800-234-5308** • _Have Your Credit Card Ready_
e-mail: info@mtnpress.com • website: www.mountain-press.com